BRICK LANE TALES

AN ANTHOLOGY OF SHORT STORIES ABOUT LONDON'S ICONIC EAST END

BY SELECTED AUTHORS

First published 2016 in the UK by Brick Lane Publishing Limited, London www.bricklanepublishing.com
1
Copyright © 2016 of the stories in this anthology belongs to their respective authors.

Authors were winners of a short story contest held by Brick Lane Publishing.

The moral right of the authors has been asserted. All rights reserved. No part of this publication may be reproduced, stored in a retrieval system or transmitted in any form or by any means, electronic, mechanical, photocopying, recording or otherwise, without the prior written permission of the publisher. All characters, events and entities in this publication, other than those clearly in the public domain, are fictitious and any resemblance to real persons, living or dead, is purely coincidental.

A CIP catalogue record for this book is available from the British Library.

TPB ISBN: 978-0-9928863-8-7

EBOOK ISBN: 978-0-9928863-9-4

Printed and bound in Great Britain by Marston Book Services Limited, Oxfordshire.

Contents

THE FACE OF '66 1

THE BELLS OF LONDON TOWN 15

THE WEIGHT OF PAPER 29

I AM IN LONDON 43

THE MAN AT THE BOOKSHOP 63

THAT DAY 73

TAKE THE LONG WAY HOME 83

BELLE'S BOWS 105

THE SQUARE 123

THE FACE OF '66

VICTORIA THOMAS

Brick Lane Tales

ABOUT THE AUTHOR

Liverpool-born Victoria has been writing since she was a child. A year studying with the poet Robert Shepherd inspired her to go on and work with the Royal Court Theatre Writer's Group and also the Liverpool Everyman Theatre.

After living in London and Paris, she completed her first novel while touring the USA as a jazz singer. Her strong interest in music and 1960s London inspired her story, *The Face of '66*. The character of Berry is inspired by photographer David Bailey after reading an article in Vogue on his career and relationship with model Jean Shrimpton. This short story was carefully researched over three months.

Brick Lane Tales

THE FIRST THING to shock me was his outfit. Skin-tight jeans, Cuban-heel boots and a little bum-freezer jacket. He was the hippest person I had ever seen, right down to the little horn-rimmed glasses hiding those eyes. I was 17. My only addictions were Woodbine Cigarettes and Acid Drop sweets.

I arrived in London the summer when the Stones were riding up the charts and mini-skirts were riding up every female behind on King's Road. On my first walk from the tube to Jane's flat, I was dizzy from turning my head to catch every sight. Jane was my guide.

"Be cool," she advised. It was something I hadn't practiced yet. I fancied myself as Julie Christie in *Darling*, when in reality I was more like Julie Andrews.

It was at Jane's that we first met. She didn't bother with chairs in the tiny apartment, forcing the Chelsea In-Crowd to huddle together among the hanging tapestries, feathers and Victorian mirrors that were her décor. A choking mix of thick smoke and perfume stuck to our throats.

I balanced against the telephone table behind a screen of peacock feathers, chain smoking. Most of Jane's friends were from Biba and *Granny Takes A Trip*, along with a few musicians. We had hopes of a visit from Dylan, as he was at the Savoy Hotel. I decided not to speak; I couldn't let it slip that I was not born within the sound of Bow Bells, and anyway, what would I say? They spoke in a new language – exotic words such as "Hulanicki" and "Quant" hung in the air like precious jewels. Furs and silks draped their wiry figures. Even the men wore make-up.

It was then that I first saw him. Every muscle trembling as he scanned the room, his eyes gleaming, head twitching; a stretched rubber band, waiting to spring. With a filthy pencil-stub, he was making strokes in a little book. Curiosity pushed me forward on the fur-covered table. We locked each other's gaze for a second and a smile cracked his face in half. He darted over and my cheeks turned crimson. What could I say? And what in the world would he want to say to me, little Carol McGuire? I drew back behind the feathers.

"You've got gorgeous eyes, darling."

What? I opened them wider as he continued to stare.

"You look like Snow White."

Was that a compliment? It sounded like one. I

suppose I *did* have a cartoon look with my huge eyes, but really. Who was this person anyway? I glanced at his stubbly beard. Had the man never heard of shaving?

He took my face in his hands and tilted it to the light. I felt my blush spreading further. I mean, what about a handshake? I braced myself for the roughness of his hands, but they were soft as he cupped my jaw. I tried not to cough at the strength of his cologne.

"Berry, put her down!" Jane crossed the room to my rescue.

He snapped out of his meditation and took my hand. "Enchanted, darlin'." He deliberately emphasised the Cockney as he did a small mock bow, then winked. "Where have you been keeping this angel, Jane? Can she act? Does she sing?"

"Carol, this is Charles Berry, the best snapper in London. Give her a chance, Berry; she's only been here a few weeks."

He circled me. I tensed as his eyes scanned up and down my body. "I think I might be able to do something with you."

I bet you can, I thought. I know your type. Auntie Ena had warned me about this sort of "flash" man. She had warned me against all men, advising that they were only after one thing.

"Get yourself to the studio at four tomorrow." He

winked again and then disappeared into a billow of Moroccan silk. Camel-scented smoke drifted back into our faces.

"Who was that? What a cocky…"

"You have to go," said Jane, gripping my sleeve. "He's a genius; he's shot the hippest people, the Stones—"

"No," I protested.

"He's incredible."

"But…"

I couldn't do it. I knew what happened in those sorts of places; photographers' studios. I'd only be there for five minutes before he would have my clothes off. I wasn't going to be taken advantage of, thank you, and certainly not that quickly.

"I'd kill for the chance," exclaimed Jane, almost shaking my arm to pieces with excitement. "He's so…"

"No."

"Yes. You have to!"

"I can't. I don't know how. It's not…"

"It is now, or never," she replied.

That was how I came to find myself outside 123 Danvers Street. If the heavily cracked paint covering the door was anything to go by, this place was nothing special. The borrowed Quant dress was displaying too much of my pale, skinny leg. People in London must be freezing all the time. He would probably see me today and completely change his mind. Pep pills had made him talk like that last night, I was sure of it. I turned, ready to walk away.

"I'm coming down, darlin'!" He had been watching me from an upstairs window. Here we go. What should I do if he tried something?

The door opened. He stood, framed. His taut jeans looked like blue-denim skin in the daylight. His shirt was a startling shade of red, brighter than the wine he was holding. He swept me up the stairs to the studio – walls of white and huge windows. Was an escape still possible? As he put *High Tide and Green Grass* on the record player, I edged towards the door. He snatched my coat and tossed it. His hands immediately went to my beehive and began rearranging my morning's work. Hairpins hit the bare wooden floor with a metallic-sounding ricochet. He pushed me towards a velvet seat in the middle of the room, tugged at my dress, almost exposing my brassiere.

"Impress me. Let's see something special."

He snatched up a camera and began to snap to the pulsating beat of the music.

"Come on then, more. That's it! No, too much. Now turn. No! No!"

He was in my face, wine breath in my mouth.

"Hair to the side – no, the other side! Face the window, to the door. Now to the window, back to the door! More! You aren't giving me magic! I need magic!"

He curved around me, shooting from all angles; bending down, then springing up with a frightening spontaneity, still shouting. This was ridiculous, I thought. I wasn't a model. They were neat and posh; they knew what to do. I was here with my dress pulled down and hair sticking up. I changed from one foot to the other. *He* didn't have to stand here half dressed.

"Leg forward." He pulled it roughly. I swayed, almost losing balance. "You're not trying! I need something! Give me something!"

I knew what I would like to give him, the bastard. He stopped as suddenly as he had started and threw his arm around me. I went to push him off. And now he was going to try and kiss me, I supposed.

"Now off with you. Get out of here!"

Was that it? One minute yelling, next he was telling me to leave.

"You're very rude." My voice echoed in the space, the Yorkshire accent coming out as it always did with anger. "You order me here; I never wanted to come. You take my hair down, my clothes off; you force me this way and that way. How dare you shout in my face like that? I've had enough of you!" I snatched up my coat as he laughed delightedly. I heard him calling out to me as I clattered down the stairs.

I told Jane exactly what had happened and what I thought of the "nice" sort of friends she had. She said I must have misunderstood him.

I was a silly fool for even going to the studio. Vanity had got the better of me, just because a famous man said I had nice eyes.

A few weeks later, I woke up and stumbled into the kitchen to make some coffee, when the telephone rang.

"I think that lovely voice belongs to Snow White if I'm not mistaken. No, don't hang up, darlin'." My hand was poised to do just that. "You need to buy the *Daily Express* today. No questions. Just go and get it."

There he went, ordering me around again. I opened my mouth to protest, but all I heard was dial tone. Unbelievable. What should I want to read in the *Daily Express*? My reading material consisted solely of *Rave* magazine and the occasional edition of *Melody Maker*. Well, I wouldn't buy it! Why should I? It was probably some story written about him, hoping to convince me he was alright after all. It was too late for that.

I finished my coffee and headed over the Albert Bridge and to my job as a typist. It was hell. This wasn't what I wanted, while the rest of London was having a gas. The people in the office were as far removed from hip as Auntie Ena. Six times each day I made Mr. Grenshaw's tea and watered a dying pot plant. The sun began to poke through the misty clouds. It would be a nice day and I'd be stuck inside with Brooke Bond tea for company. Why wasn't I Jane with straight blonde hair and a boyfriend in a band?

I headed towards the station, trying to ignore the wafting aroma of espresso from Cafe Picasso. I fumbled in my handbag, my hand closing around a cold shilling piece. The packet of Woodbines in there felt too light. That would never do, I could not get through a day of Mr. Grenshaw without cigarettes. I turned to retrace my steps. A stack of newspapers stood outside a corner shop. I supposed it wouldn't do me any harm to see if they were the *Daily Express*. Maybe it would be a good thing to find out what Berry had wanted me to read. My eyes darted around the shop. There it was, the *Daily Express*, on a shelf. Without troubling to pay, I picked it up and scanned the front page headline: "Moor's Murderers Jailed for Life". Was it that? Was that what he was talking about? I flicked the paper open and began rustling through the pages, one after another, squinting in the poorly-lit shop.

The man behind the counter boomed, "This ain't a bloody library, sweetheart, you buy that or you put it down!"

I barely heard him. There, spread across a full page was my face! My eyes looked huge and my lips were slightly parted, as if in surprise. But why? I read the half-inch size print under the image: "The New Face of Swinging London." I almost stopped breathing. That was *me*. In the newspaper, not even just as a model. As The New Face of Swinging London. You couldn't get more hip than that! I gathered up copies. One for me, Jane, Auntie Ena – I'll just take the lot, who needs cigarettes! I threw all of my change onto the counter; shouts came from behind me as I ran out into the street. What had happened? Who had written this? And why? So many questions, but they didn't matter now. I was going to be famous! Maybe I was already being recognised. And I knew who to thank, damn him!

THE BELLS OF LONDON TOWN

TABITHA POTTS

ABOUT THE AUTHOR

Tabitha grew up just around the corner from Brick Lane and has lived in East London for years. She has always found the people, architecture and history of the area to be constant sources of creative inspiration. One such is the chiming church bells near where she lives – the Bells of Stepney mentioned in *Oranges and Lemons*, a nursery rhyme that features as a reference point for her short story. She once took a tour of the bell tower to see the belfry and the ringing room where the ringers are hidden from view, almost like a secret society.

She wrote about a rogue trader because the nursery rhyme itself is about earning, owing and spending money. Londoners have been trading for centuries and Tabitha wanted to explore that theme further. Her day job is managing and editing websites, and she's fascinated by technology and the internet, but finds herself thinking about legends, ghosts, and old stories when she sets to creative writing.

I AM A campanologist. That is to say, a student in the ancient art of ringing church bells. It's been several years since this pastime, I suppose you would call it, entered my life.

It had been a long day in the glass tower in Canary Wharf where I'm based. I've given up telling people what I do for a living as their eyes tend to glaze over with boredom, but yes, I make myself, and my bank, a lot of money.

I had been staring at my screens since 5 a.m. It felt as if I hadn't blinked even once. Come evening, my eyes felt dry and gritty.

"How's it going?" asked Joe Wharton, a trader who sits at a desk immediately adjacent to mine and for whom I have a particular distaste. His smug smile suggested he'd had a good day.

"Not bad," I said, with an equally smug expression, inviting him to guess on my fortunes that day. We both knew how turbulent the markets had been for the past few hours, which meant that profits as well as losses could be amplified quickly. I grabbed my coat and made for the office door before Wharton could press the matter any further and drive a conversation towards our bonus payments, which were due in a month's time. Although I was one of the firm's star traders, he was snapping at my heels and evidently saw me as some kind of competition.

I decided to walk home from Canary Wharf, starting on the Thames path to Limehouse. Sometimes, I would hear echoes of old London as I listened to the tidal slap and suck at the water's edge, though all around me was visual evidence of the 21st century, with its sleek towers, glittering facades and corporate self-promotion.

Leaving the River Thames pathway near the Grapes pub, I decided on an impulse to walk up from Limehouse towards my home in Shoreditch. I liked to walk around London in the evenings, when the shadows softened and changed the appearance of the buildings. Trying out this new route, I cut through the marina and across Commercial Road, and after a short time, I heard church bells ringing.

Following the sound of the chimes through Stepney Green, I came to a beautiful old church and yard, incongruous among the modern parks and tower blocks. A solitary raven posed theatrically on top of a graffiti-smeared monument, and beyond the bird there seemed to be no one around. It began to rain – at first a few drops and then suddenly a downpour – so I sheltered in the entrance of the church, which, while well-lit, also appeared to be empty.

The ringing stopped abruptly and a casually-dressed man, clearly not the Vicar, walked out into the nave and caught sight of me standing by the open doors.

"Are you here for the practice?" he asked.

I don't know why I said yes, but I did. I normally only talked to strangers when I was out clubbing, drinking and getting high, but on this occasion, I was intrigued. He asked me to follow him, and soon I was standing in the bell ringing chamber of St. Dunstan's, where he invited me to help ring rounds, a simple sequence of bells played between treble and tenor.

Arthur, the man who'd just invited me to join him, explained how the system worked. "English bells are not chimed, but rather rung," he said. "Each bell is mounted on a wheel facing upwards and the ringer must rotate the bell in a full circle by pulling a rope."

I have a good ear for music and fast reactions, but it is much harder to ring the bell at the right moment than it initially appears, especially given the physical exertion and precise timing it requires.

We began with ringing a "round" and then embarked on "call-change" ringing, which occurs when the sequence of the bells is altered and the changes are called out. I was only starting to get it right at the end of two hours' fairly constant practice. It suited me; my life as a trader also required fast reactions, with focus and calm under pressure. I knew I'd be able to do it well if I put my mind to it.

In the pub afterwards, Arthur told me more about the ringers. I learned how they played in different churches all over the East End, but this church was a favourite because of the quality of its bells and the fact they had a peal of ten bells – more than usual.

"St. Dunstan's is one of the churches from the nursery rhyme," he said in hushed tones, as if imparting some great secret. "All of the churches in that rhyme are near to or in the old City of London." He leaned a little closer. With his beard and round glasses, he was the sort of person that most would immediately class as eccentric and harmless, with a penchant for real ale and a passion for stamp collecting or bird watching. Arthur's obsession, of course, was bells.

"The Bow bells – at St. Mary-le-Bow in Cheapside – were rung as a curfew every evening until the nineteenth century," he continued. "In fact, it was the sound of the Bow Bells that persuaded Dick Whittington to turn around and come back to London. And the bell of Old Bailey refers to the great bell at St. Sepulchre-without-Newgate opposite the Old Bailey, which rung every time a prisoner was executed. Newgate was a prison for debtors and for criminals, which is why the bell's words in the rhyme are, 'When will you pay me?'" He lowered his voice a little. "Bells are the heartbeat of this city. Sometimes I imagine if the bells stopped ringing, the city would stop forever."

RECENTLY I'VE BEEN working longer and longer. As a trader, it's possible to make a lot of money, but that means routinely taking on a heck of a lot of risk and being in the office all hours. This means I don't have time for much else than work. However, I am bell ringing at least once a week now, usually when the financial markets are closed, and whenever else I can, really.

I don't know why I find my new pastime so satisfying, but I undeniably do. Perhaps I am helping to keep the city's heart beating, or is it the sheer thrill I get from ringing a pitch-perfect peal? Peals are when you are able to ring changes continuously, with a minimum of 5,000 changes. A peal must be "true" in that there must be no repetition of any change throughout. I love the idea that truth and falsity can be so readily determined in bell ringing. I could ring peals all day if I had the time.

My name is now in the peal book at St. Leonard's, Shoreditch, where there are 12 bells for "change" ringing. I learned that this was another of the nursery rhyme churches when I saw the mailbox for "Oranges and Lemons letters" whose final destination this is. Shoreditch bells in the nursery rhyme say, "When I grow rich" because the area was so poor; at one point the church had to raise money to build a workhouse for the parish.

It's certainly changed now. My place in Shoreditch cost a fortune. I bought it outright after last year's bonus payment, and in this market, the value can only go up as far as I can see. I definitely see the property as an investment.

There's a girl among the ringers, called Sara. She was talking to me about the spiraling property prices in East London and what it means for locals. Apparently they're getting priced off the market and have to buy cheaper properties farther out. I told her that prices going up will mean more money moving into the area, and eventually it will improve housing stock, schools and retail provision.

Twenty years ago, this area was awful, I told her, and it would have stayed that way if people like her had their way. By that I meant it would have still been full of crime, unemployment and people living on benefits. She asked me what I did for a living and when I told her, she gave a broad smile. "That makes sense."

She was a lot better looking than you might expect, so I asked if she wanted to join me at my favourite club in London, where the whole dance floor applauds if you buy a magnum of champagne. She declined. Her loss. She probably would have had the best night out in her life, or at least that's what I told myself. Lately, I've tended to go shopping for women on the internet. You get to have a good look before you "buy." There's a huge amount of choice; guaranteed high quality if you don't mind paying the price, and best of all, you can send them back.

ARTHUR TOLD ME that one of the other churches named in the long version of the nursery rhyme, St. Botolph's, was in an area infamous for prostitution and it was called the prostitute's church. *Old Father Baldpate,* ring out the slow bells of Aldgate in the rhyme. Old Father Baldpate is a reference to Saint Botolph's tonsure, or possibly something slightly further down his torso. But it all comes back to money. That's what I think the bells of London sing about.

Arthur sees it altogether differently. He believes that ringing church bells bring people together. They were rung to celebrate God, or mark a christening, wedding, or funeral. There were harvest bells and gleaning bells to let you know when to start and finish work. There was a bell to let you know when you were allowed to visit Bedlam, the asylum in Bishopsgate. Bells were supposed to protect you against fire, plague, and the devil, which is why they were rung when someone died, to save their soul.

THINGS ARE GETTING very tense at work. I know the ever-smarmy Wharton is watching me closely and I'm worried he might try and stitch me up for taking on too much risk and keeping it quiet. I know the bank won't care if I cut corners, so long as I make a tidy profit at the end of it all. On the other hand, the bosses will deny all knowledge if I get it wrong. I'm not the first in this situation and I almost certainly won't be the last. Anyway, despite the massive loss showing on my account, I've got some trading tactics that I know will turn it all around. For sure. After all, I understand the market better than anyone.

It was 4 a.m. and I'd been doing an all-nighter at work trying to sort things out – with the help of a few lines to clear my head – when I heard something unusual. I can recognise the sound of bells, any time of day or night. There aren't too many and my ears are attuned to them. There's so much noise pollution that people say you can only hear the Bow Bells in the City and Shoreditch nowadays.

What I heard was a peal that comprised at least twelve individual bells and had some changes that I just couldn't work out. It was coming from a different direction to all the local bell towers and I couldn't place it. I went for a walk to see where these beautiful, compelling chimes were coming from. It's really not hard to follow the bells once you're accustomed to being guided by your ears. I ended up in a place by the river that I hadn't seen before. It's strange to think I'd been working here for so long and hadn't noticed it. There were hardly any lights on the street, just the dark, still water, and it was so late that I couldn't see much beyond the general outlines of buildings. But the sound of the bells was getting closer all the time.

I GET MORE than my 15 minutes of fame and even find myself on the TV news: "Mysterious disappearance of rogue trader ... Bank could go under – trader missing." The headlines are many and varied.

When interviewed, Wharton describes me as seeming "ill and preoccupied" when he last saw me. Once they start checking the bank's balance sheet and see the damage done, there is an easy explanation. Some people might think I've ended up on a sunny beach somewhere, grinning over a lurid cocktail. Could have happened – there were plenty of cash withdrawals from my own bank account, as well as a lot of over-spending on the corporate credit card, and perhaps it didn't all go up my nose. Of course the police drag the river for me, but the Thames hugs her secrets tightly and nothing's surfaced so far. What people see when they watch the security camera footage on TV – the last recorded moment of my life – is my walking under and then away from the street light, as though I briefly flicker under its illumination and then am swallowed completely by the darkness of the city around me. I become one with it, as if I have never been anything else.

Police say a search of the area is still underway.

THE WEIGHT OF PAPER

SARAH EVANS

ABOUT THE AUTHOR

Sarah Evans has had over a hundred stories published in anthologies, magazines, and online, with outlets including: Bridport Prize, Unthank Books, Lighthouse, Structo, and Best New Writing. She has won a number of short story prizes, including Words and Women, Winston Fletcher, Stratford Literary Festival, Glass Woman, and Rubery. She has also had work performed in London, Hong Kong, and New York.

Her story *The Weight of Paper* was inspired by her great-great-grandfather. Of Russian Jewish origin, he fled the pogroms in the late 1800s and emigrated to London, where he settled in the East End and set up a tobacconist shop. This story is, however, fiction.

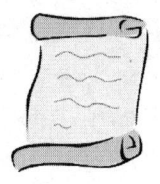

THE AIR IS sharp as Yacob steps outside the house, its grand frontage rising high to the attic rooms that he and his family occupy. Frost glitters on the windows and Yacob holds himself close, exhaling white mist, though it is never really cold here. His neck chafes against a new collar and he scratches his chin through the softness of a freshly trimmed beard.

He walks briskly, the cobbles hard through his good boots, heading south towards the river, keeping east. Already, the close-pressed roads are filled with those pushing laden barrows towards the market or heading towards the docks. The guttural music of his mother tongue is gaily shouted, and the air is thick with the tang of pickled herring and onion bread. On another morning, he might stop to exchange greetings, but he has no time to linger – not today.

He passes number 19, and from the outside it could be just one more abode where many families dwell. Through the house, the garden is built into a synagogue. Each Sabbath he congregates there, vying for elbow room within the tiny space that is rendered sacred by the housing of heavy scrolls, which – like those gathered – have survived their passage over the seas. The men sing and wail, they laugh and cry, and amidst the fervour, they could almost think themselves back home.

He twists and turns along narrow streets – Princes Street, Wilkes, Fournier, Commercial – a zigzag path that brings him closer to his destination. Reaching Whitechapel, the road opens out, stinking of soot and horse-dung. He hears the peal of Bow Bells ringing and he knows that he is close to entering the centre of commerce and administration. His eyes alight on a sign, Jewry Street, and inwardly he smiles; his kind have been here for many years.

He draws level with the building he seeks, with its red bricks and fancy stone façade, and he keeps to the other side of the road. The doors are not yet open, though already people huddle, clutching papers to them, vying to be first in line.

He steps back into a doorway for the passing of a cart. He is a big man, broad-chested, but he knows how to disappear. With his fair hair, its curls constrained under a wide-brimmed hat, he is not easily recognisable. It is only when he speaks. He has worked hard to master this foreign tongue, studying it by night, using up good candles through the hours of darkness. But it is his voice that states he does not belong here.

Until today.

A pale glow slowly fills the windows opposite. The wooden doors open, just a crack at first, and the people snap alert. Yacob moves to join them, careful to keep out of the way of those who hurry along the street, their shoulders hunched against the trifling winter of this place. He thinks of being one of them, a man like any other.

"Think of it, Roza," he had said. "*Equal under the law.*" The law is not everything, he knows that; it does not control the hearts of men. But it is a good place to start.

Roza had pursed her lips. She hasn't said it, but he knows what she thinks: *The laws of man can change.*

The cluster of men – some of his tribe, others not – are ushered inside those solid walls containing centuries of history, their own together with the stories of those who pass through the intricately carved doors. They are told to form a single queue that shuffles towards a wooden desk, with its stern-faced clerks.

At his waist, he feels the stone-weight of coins in the leather pouch tied to his belt. He has documents, too, carefully laid in a black folder. Signed testimonies – the manager at the bank who recently extended him a loan, the owner of a haberdashery – all assert he is a fine and upright man. The words are prescribed, but still his heart swells. They are his invitation to stay, from those whose roots grow deep in the earth of this land.

Ahead of him is some sort of commotion, a man protesting, half in English, half in his own tongue, whatever that is. The clerk insists that the man's papers are not sufficient.

"No," he says, the word echoing like a gunshot. "No. I must ask you to leave."

Yacob holds his own documents closer.

"You, sir." The second clerk's voice is abrupt, unnecessarily so, but Yacob does not react as he steps meekly forward. There is no seat, so he must stand as he answers the questions asked of him, his responses transcribed in dark ink.

He does not offer his father's name. "No one can pronounce it," he had argued with Roza, "everyone writes it wrongly. What is in a name? It is still my forefathers' blood."

Today Yakob Leibowicz will become Jacob Lewis.

The pen scratches the document and now Roza's name lies beneath his, followed by the names of their three boys.

Abram grows like his father, tall and strong, and he comes in from the streets with bruises he refuses to explain. At night he sweats and cries out.

David is quiet, except for his endlessly questioning, "*Why?*"

"A rabbi," his mother whispers her fond hopes.

Elias, the youngest, is like the sun coming up, spreading a smile wherever he is.

"That is all?" the clerk asks, and Yacob nods, though a fourth child grows. *Let it be a girl.* He dare not pray for it, lest it seem ungrateful. God has already granted much. But this time, he hopes for a girl.

The clerk demands to check the contents of the purse, testing the coins one by one, each with so many competing demands.

"Your documents?"

Yacob's heart falters as he places his folder down, the contents much weightier than the leaves of paper, fearful he will be discovered lacking, missing something. He knows those eyes that barely glance at him, the contempt they hold, speaking that he is not welcome. His shoulders push back, straight and square. People can look all they like. They will not spit, there will be no blows, they will not come with uncovered faces in the night to take what is not theirs, while the law looks on and condones.

The clerk shuffles and reshuffles the papers that tell only an outline of Yacob's story, skimming over the long, heart-heavy route that has brought him here.

Leaving their home. Bidding farewell to those they love. Facing the treachery of the wide ocean and of those they had paid to bring them here. Two weeks after they had landed, he finally understood: the men who took his money for onwards passage to America had disappeared.

"It is God's will," he had persuaded Roza, so that he too might bend to God's plans and believe in the promise of this place.

London was full of hostile stares, with small pockets of human kindness. They settled amidst their own and at first it might almost have seemed as if they had not left the shtetl. Slowly, they put down roots. He learned his trade in tobacco, hauling great sacks on the docks from dawn to dusk, while Roza worked among the women, their light fingers turning the dried leaf into cigarettes. He saved what little he could. He set his hopes on the high seas and prayed for his investment to come back.

Though the shop was rented, when that day finally arrived and he weighed the hefty keys in his hand, it felt like his own. He was proud to become a shopkeeper in this land of them.

Yacob's clientele come for the quality of his produce, for his impeccable service. He knows the feel and smell of brown leaf, of fine cigars. He drives a hard bargain.

Jew, they call him, filling the word with scorn. But the word states what he is. And his family is safe at night, save for Abram, who still wakes with the smell of burning in his mouth and the wails of women in his ears.

The clerk reassembles the documents roughly, the edges creasing. He gives no indication as to whether the affairs of this Jew are in order.

"Wait." His hand waves to the side in dismissal.

Yacob smoothes and tidies his papers. They show how his business prospers. A shop for each of his sons is what he dreams of. And perhaps for daughters, too, should God find it fitting to grant his wish.

His feet shift, unused to idleness, but a little more waiting is nothing; he has waited seven years already. He catches the cold, blue eyes of the clerk as he calls the next man forward.

Seven years…

Before, he never wanted girls. When the mobs came, it was not just belongings they stole and broke, not just men they beat and killed. What they did to the women was worse.

Afterwards, he and Roza could not look at one another. His eyes burned into the earth floor with impotent fury. Roza's dress was torn, her eyes empty and she kept her head bowed while she swept up the shards of glass in the room, where all they'd built had been destroyed. That night she crept beside Abram.

Yacob's bruised body lay on the bare ground and ached with wanting, just to hold her. Night after night, she stayed away while her belly swelled. The months passed with no whispering of names. She did not pull his hand to her to share the strength of the baby's kick.

After this, his days of labour were harder and the cold of winter bit more harshly. Life had turned to ice without the melting ring of laughter from the girl he had shyly married, though they had not previously exchanged more than a few words. At night, he lay awake, shivering against the emptiness. Each time, they had told themselves, *this is the worst*. Each time, they bowed to the mass of regulations, rules, laws that circumscribed their lesser lives, carving out a small space for themselves, in which they might finally be free to exist.

The men gathered to talk. But what can a man do against a madness that says it is the victims who are at fault for the incitement to hatred?

The birth was long and difficult. He prayed as he had never prayed before, "Let her live."

The cries carried on, and the bowls of bloodied water poured from the closed room, their metallic tang of death. He searched to find what he could offer up to the God who had seemingly abandoned him, until, worn out, he prayed, "Let her live. Let both of them live."

He heard the first feeble squawk. The midwife opened the door. "A boy."

Roza lay exhausted, her eyes finally searching his, and through her daze of pain he read fragile stirrings of hope.

He looked down at the swaddled bundle. The child opened his gaze on the newly created world.

"He has his mother's eyes." He dared not examine the features too closely. Miniature fingers reached up and unfurled, opening a place in his heart, and he rested his own finger in their midst, feeling the strength of that tiny grip.

After eight days had passed, he took the child and carried him to the synagogue for the ritual cut, which would mark him out.

His race has learned to survive. They have learned to bend with the violent torrent and not break, accepting what cannot be changed: lineage is passed down through the mother. And if God accepted this child as one of His Chosen, who was Yacob to deny him.

Afterwards, the men gathered round, clasping his arm, offering muted congratulations. *Mazel Tov*. Roza's father held back to be the last. He grasped Yacob by the shoulder. "I will help." Voicing the thoughts Yacob had not yet spoken.

That night, Roza came to lie beside him, still wearied and torn, and he whispered the plans that had twisted and turned in his mind for nine months. "When you're strong again, when the baby's bigger, we'll go somewhere safe."

HIS NAME IS called. He shakes himself. Today is not for dwelling on the past. He is led into a panelled room. The official is grandly dressed and his face contains an expression of ceremonial courtesy, in which Yacob ascertains that his application is granted. As he speaks the words he has memorised, the oath of allegiance to this new country in which he swears by his own God, Yacob feels his insides pressing outwards, as if there is not enough room for so much hope. The official suppresses a yawn, this ritual of words and signings, the exchange of coins for rights, rendered dull by repetition. He adds his seal to the papers.

Soon Jacob is outside, eyes squinting into a pale sun, his purse empty. His hand clutches the flimsy piece of paper, whose ink states his naturalisation as a British citizen.

Roza had grumbled at the cost, her hand resting on the swell of her belly, her dark eyes still harbouring fear. She would prefer him to squirrel away insurance for when – once again – they might have to move on.

But today he has willingly offered up his surety, exchanging his labour of many days for nothing more than a promise.

It is his pledge of trust in his adopted land, his trust in freedom.

I AM IN LONDON

RAHAD ABIR

ABOUT THE AUTHOR

Born and bred in Dhaka, Bangladesh, Rahad Abir is a fiction writer. His short stories have appeared in *The Penmen Review, Toad Suck Review, Aerodrome, Blue Lyra Review, and New Asian Writing*. He has worked as journalist, university teacher, and interpreter. Currently he is working on a novel.

Rahad lived in London for about three years, from 2009 to 2012. This story is based on his London experience.

ARRIVING AT HEATHROW Airport made Robiul fidgety. He'd been waiting a very long time to pass the immigration desk. Back home, he'd heard a few unpleasant stories, where immigration officers would refuse entry to anyone they were not satisfied with, even if that passenger had a visa.

Robiul had graduated with a degree in English and could speak the language just fine, or so he thought. He hoped it would be an advantage right now. In the first-time visitor queue, he tried being cool, but it was with damp palms he clutched the necessary papers.

Why are you taking this course?

If I achieve this diploma that's leading to MBA, I'd get a very good job and salary when I'm back in my country. A British degree is highly…

But you've studied English, so what good is an MBA?

Well…

He wondered if he would come across that last question. It was tricky, but his answers were prepared.

Finally, his turn came. The officer was forty-ish; a red-faced man with thinning blond hair. Robiul handed over his passport and tuberculosis certificate.

"Where did you get the money for your course?" The officer looked him over.

"I worked as a teacher; I saved the money," Robiul answered confidently.

The officer stamped his passport, handed it back with his right hand, and held the little entry gate open with his left.

Was that all? Robiul looked at the officer, then at the gate.

"Thank you," he said after a moment. He clenched his fist and quietly punched the air. "Yes, I am in London."

IT WAS THE name. He had to do it. He was, after all, in London. His flatmate had taken him to Stratford to open a bank account. When their turn came, he heard his flatmate's name being called.

"My-boob." A red-haired young woman with plump breasts smiled at them from her seat.

They sank to the sofa before her desk. She looked comfortable, and so did his flatmate, Mahboob. Robiul's face flamed red. Because of the

"Britishisation" of Mahboob, the "h" had become silent. It should have been pronounced *"Maahh-boob."* He gazed determinedly at the freckles on her forehead.

In that moment, he decided to "Britishise" his name, shortening Robiul to Rob. In fact, if possible, he would legally change his entire name, Mohammed Robiul, to Rob Ryan. The religious group he was born into had a particular fondness for naming their male children either Abdul or Mohammed. And, quite unlike his home country, where people were called by their last names, the British preferred being addressed by their first names.

Later, when he figured out how long the legal name-changing procedure would take and the effort involved, he was horrified. Still, he didn't wish to run the risk of the Home Office pushing him into a darkened room for a prolonged interrogation as a suspected Islami terrorist.

"Call me Rob," he introduced himself.

THE FIRST FEW weeks brought unexpected challenges. Rob found his eyes drifting helplessly to women's cleavages and their near-naked thighs. It took months for him to get used to the many and varied displays of female flesh. Still, he would strip off his newcomer outfit sooner than most. He had to.

One afternoon, he popped into a small

Bangladeshi store on Brick Lane to top up his travel card. When done, Rob pointed to the yoghurt in the refrigerator and asked, "How much is it?"

The shopkeeper, a young lad with a skin fade haircut and chinstrap beard – very common in Sylheti folk – replied, "Ten quid." With a bit of a condescending smile he added, "Can you afford it?"

"I'll come back later," Rob abruptly left the shop. He hadn't quite grasped the shopkeeper's question. For someone fresh off the boat, the British accent was tough. Most certainly, Sylheti-cockney was no exception, if not the worst of all accents to understand. But, there had been something needling about the shopkeeper's manner.

What exactly did he mean? Rob pondered as he walked the grimy footpath. Understanding dawned. He stopped and spat on the concrete.

THE FIRST DAY of college arrived in a two-floor section of a multi-story building located at Holborn. In orientation class it occurred to Rob that he might well have travelled back in time to 1947, when Bangladesh, India, and Pakistan were all part of the same country.

He watched the other students. He noticed something: everyone was of Indian heritage. There were no exceptions, not even the teachers and school employees.

Am I really in London?

Back home, he had often imagined himself in a foreign school, surrounded by students from every corner of the globe. Different races, languages and cultures – the idea had always thrilled him. He eyes roamed the faces in the room as he waited expectantly for a flicker of excitement. Nothing. A skeletal girl of indeterminate age stared back at him. She looked ordinary, worn, mundane. Rob sighed.

Relief was overwhelming when he later left the classroom. Diverse faces passed around him on the frenetic streets outside. It was oddly comforting.

WHITECHAPEL AND ITS surrounding areas had the biggest Bengali community in London. There, Rob visited a few agencies he'd heard could help him find a job. The small, stuffy rooms, always heaving, were damp and dirty. In almost every office the person in charge was chewing betel nut, against a backdrop of peeling walls. They never missed an opportunity to take advantage of hapless jobseekers, preferably by skimming hefty commissions in return for "services." Rob soon gave up on them.

One evening, on a friend's recommendation, he landed a work trial at an Indian restaurant in central London. While he confidently balanced a tray of bottled Kingfisher beer in one hand, he had, for a fleeting moment, imagined himself as a real waiter.

Placing the drinks on the table, the tray tilted; one by one the Kingfishers slid off, saturating the girl's top and puckering her pale skin. He was invited to leave.

Feeling miserable, he slunk to Soho, where Mahboob worked at a small book shop.

"It's hard to get a job these days," Mahboob tried to soothe him. "Keep trying, bro. You never know."

Rob gazed intently at some of the books. Due to the shop's location, it shelved a wide range of adult reading. His eyes fell on one title: *The Big Book of Pussy*. It reminded him of the words of a fellow student, a Pakistani, who had warned him to stay away from British women, because they apparently used their pets for erotic pleasure. He ached to clarify this point with Mahboob, who was by then serving a customer. Instead, Rob found himself hating the dogs that received repeated sweet kisses from adorable, full-lipped women.

When he had finished, Mahboob sighed. "This is London life," he said, "look at me, six years I've been here and still I'm effing studying."

"Why is that?"

"Well, I have to. I don't wanna go back to that country. Just four more years, bro. I'll get my residency and no more effing school then."

A MONTH PASSED, and Rob landed a cleaning job in central London through an English job-seeking agency. In the interview, the Latvian cleaning manager – a bone-thin, blonde, freckled woman, in her mid-thirties – asked a single question in a strange accent, "Do you have cleaning job experience?"

He was candid. "Not exactly," was his reply, "but at home, I clean my own toilet."

He woke at 5:20 a.m. to start work at 6 a.m. at the largest department store on Oxford Street. The job mainly involved sweeping, mopping and vacuuming. The morning shift lasted three hours and his second shift began at 3 p.m.. Most of his co-workers were Filipino, who spoke broken English. Four Bangladeshis were among them, newcomers like him. Soon, he found himself chatting to a young Bangladeshi man with a thoughtful face, who was assumed to be a well-brought-up city boy. On their way home, the city boy, hands in his pockets, stopped in the middle of the pavement. His eyes widened when Rob spoke of his education and qualification.

"You got a master's from the best university back home, why the hell have you come here? To do this shit job?"

"I wanted a change, and I love to travel." Rob did his best to sound convincing.

"I was doing my bachelor's from a no-good university," the city boy said. "And I know I won't get a good job there. So, I came to London to make my fortune." He paused to inspect one of Oxford

Street's Christmas decorations, and added, "But I get your point."

Rob gave a tight smile.

COLLEGE WAS A bore after two weeks. There were three courses and three teachers: a Bangladeshi, an Indian and a newly-employed Ghanaian. Staying interested in class was a struggle, and their ever-changing accents irked Rob. At the British Council back home, he'd encountered what he considered to be "proper" British instructors. A longing to get under the skin of this cold and foreign land gnawed at him.

It was with relief that the college closed for Christmas holidays. The department store had become busier by the minute and he was offered plenty of hours, usually from 6 a.m. to 9 p.m., which he grabbed. Rob soon found himself either on his feet at work, or at home in bed. The department store became his second home. At night, when he arrived at the flat and found his bed, he crawled under the covers and slept like the dead.

On his days off, Rob called his parents back home. Conversations were short and more or less same.

"It's too busy here. I'm good, working hard. I'll send some money next week. Don't worry about my loan."

"Do you like working in the restaurant?" they

asked. When it came to his employment situation, Rob was sketchy.

"It's okay. You get free food at the end of the shift."

He yawned and stretched for a while. Finally, from the warmth of the quilt, he rose to his feet. He cooked, washed and cleaned the flat he shared with four other guys. His balding roommate joked, "Today our kitchen and toilet will be super clean."

After taking his meal, Rob returned to his den, curling up under the quilt.

Calling Rob, over.

Yes, Rob speaking, over.

Rob, can you go to Godiva now? A customer threw up on the floor. Over.

OK, I'm on my way.

Thank you, Rob.

His eyes shot open and he weakly flailed about, before realising he wasn't at work. Had he taken a walkie-talkie home by mistake? He was resting in his best cosy place on earth. Where had these instructions come from? Would he not have the pleasure to enjoy his day off? Working in a huge six-story department store with more than twenty other cleaners, who were constantly scurrying around with non-stop talking radios, had made his entire world seem as if it were under walkie-talkie range. Rob sighed and closed his eyes. He needed sleep.

It must've been a miracle. The next day when he was assigned to the ground floor, an instruction crackled over the radio.

"Rob, please make your way to the beauty section," the voice said.

"On my way. Over," Rob answered.

It was a vomit mess by the Jo Malone till. The shop manager and the floor manager encircled the spot to alert other customers. The unfortunate woman who had puked was still there, repeatedly saying sorry. The floor manager responded with her best game face.

"It's okay, don't worry about it." She smiled. She looked stunning in her black dress. Her soft wavy hair was shining; her long French-manicured nails were gleaming. Today she smelled of an oriental fragrance. Warm, spicy, and intense. Rob would have been the happiest person on earth if he could slap her polished face right then.

It's okay? Cleaning this shit is okay?

THE FIRST WEEK of January arrived and work resumed a more normal pace. At last, there was more time for Rob to catch up on sleep, and to surf the internet. To his satisfaction, while searching for jobs one evening, he stumbled across an online dating site.

Lonely, and in need of someone to warm his body and soul, he signed up then and there. Flicking through women's profiles quickly became his favourite pastime; it was incredibly exciting that scores of them were seeking male company at any given time. Within two weeks he had hooked up with an English girl, Lauren, whose profile stated she was "interested in Asian guys."

Their first date took place at a Weatherspoon pub. It was a Wednesday evening, and the brunette sitting opposite him appeared much older than he, average looking and a little overweight. She was wearing a red, V-neck top that displayed her cleavage, light blue jeans and kitten-heel shoes.

"So, how do you find London?" was her opening gambit.

"It's good," he said animatedly. "But life's harder here."

"I know. I've been made redundant. I feel it every day."

He caught the whiff of a familiar fragrance; Jasmine and roses.

"Are you wearing Chanel?" he asked.

She was flabbergasted. "How do you know?"

"Just guessing." The amazement in her almond eyes pleased him.

"I like Merlot," she said, gazing steadily at him.

"I like Tuborg," he said, taking a draft.

They stared at each other.

"You're so young," she hissed.

They smoked cigarettes, drank some more, and talked until the Victorian clock at the pub showed half past ten. They put their overcoats on, and side-by-side, made for the door. Outside, in the middle of the walkway, she gave him a hearty goodbye kiss.

Three days later, Lauren's father died and much to Rob's dismay, she left immediately for her hometown in Surrey. Meeting her had numbed his vague fear of being taken advantage of, acquired upon his arrival in the country. He had finally discovered someone with whom he could experience actual *Britishness*. With the exploratory enthusiasm of stepping forth into a fresh, new land, he strained to see England as the British had once viewed India through their English eyes. With Lauren, he'd had a sense of having struck a rich seam of discovery.

A month later, Lauren returned. That weekend, they arranged to meet at the Weatherspoon pub of their first date, which was not far from her flat. They ate dinner and split the bill. She invited him to her flat for a drink. He accepted.

Her two-bed flat in East London faced the local park. Orange streetlight dimly filled the drawing room from the big window behind the sofa, creating an illusory image. Rob watched her open a kitchen cupboard, take down a bottle of red wine, and pour two glasses. They sat on the floor with their backs against the sofa. The flat was simple and warm, and her easy-going company was pleasant. That night, Rob stayed over. The next Sunday, he stayed again. And so began a weekly routine.

Rob liked it there. Just the two of them, drinking wine, smoking cigarettes, watching a film, eating dinner. Only one thing depressed Lauren, and it was that they rarely went out as a couple.

One day she asked, "Are you ashamed of me when we go out, Rob?"

"Oh no," he said. "What makes you think that?"

"Sometimes, I feel far away, and I don't really see an attachment," she said, looking straight at him. "Is it the language barrier?"

He looked blankly at her.

SIX MONTHS LATER, Rob and Lauren were having a serious conversation.

"I can't stand it anymore," Rob said. "The college is crap."

"What do you want to do then?" Her eyes were compassionate.

"I dunno. A university here costs a hell of a lot of money. I don't earn that much." He let out a sigh. "I wish I were not here. What have I got here? Crap job. Crap college. Crap life."

"Nope, you forgot the most precious thing," she

blurted out. She fastened her eyes on Rob, waiting to hear something. "You got me." She laughed.

"Oh yes, sorry." He gave a quick smile.

She picked up his hand. It was dry. Hers was soft and warm. "Hun, I don't know when I'll get a job again. I'm paying my mortgage, you know. But if you need it, I can lend you a small amount."

"Lauren, you're really something. You really are." Rob leaned forward and crossed one leg over the other. "But you know what, I feel I'm lost. Too many restrictions on foreign students. And at the end of the day, the idea of being a permanent resident seems out of the question."

"Sweetie, don't get disappointed. I'm here with you, okay? Look, if the worst comes to the worst, we can get married."

Rob stared at Lauren as if she were not the woman she was before.

"I'm serious. I mean it."

"I know," Rob said softly. He fell silent. After a while, he got up and moved towards the toilet.

In the sofa again, he sat by the window, crossed his legs, and observed her for a moment. He then said he'd forgotten to tell her that he had a job tomorrow morning. Someone had cancelled the shift, so he had been asked to cover. This simply implied he wouldn't spend the night, and that he should take his leave.

Her calm and fair face slowly changed. "This is ridiculous." Her nostrils flared.

She lit a cigarette, turning her face towards the window. Rob looked down at the floor, his hands in his lap. He didn't want her to feel abandoned.

He was home by 10:30 p.m., but lay wakefully in bed until roughly three in the morning. It was late when he got up, almost lunchtime. He didn't have a job today. He had lied to Lauren and didn't know why.

In the kitchen, Mahboob was having a late breakfast.

"Hey, whassup, bro?" Mahboob greeted him. "Why you here today?"

Rob opened the refrigerator door and closed it without taking anything out. "Umm," he gazed at Mahboob's half-eaten banana. "Bro, I made a big decision last night. I'm going back to Dhaka."

"What? Is everything alright?"

"Absolutely. Everything is fine in Dhaka and in London. It's just me only."

"Why then? You've not even been here for a year."

Rob took a long breath. "When I left Dhaka, I was confused. I was lost. But now I know what to do with my life."

"Are you serious?"

"I don't believe that wasting too much time and energy for years to live in this country can be someone's goal in life. It's not worth it." Rob then told Mahboob about Lauren saying she would be happy to marry him to change his immigration status.

Mahboob gaped at him for a moment. Then he cried, "You fool, man. Just marry her, move into her flat, get the passport and then throw her away. Who cares?"

"That's just wrong," Rob said.

"Man!" Mahboob banged his fist on the table. "The British have eaten us alive for two hundred years. You just eat one old chicken."

A familiar feeling tugged at Rob, and a restless smile spread across his face. That elusive thing he'd been searching for was at last defined. He knew where he belonged.

THE MAN AT THE BOOKSHOP

KATE BONYNGE

ABOUT THE AUTHOR

Kate Bonynge works in theatre by day and by night she is a freelance article writer. She is an avid people-watcher. This is her first published story.

The inspiration came from her personal experience in and around Brick Lane and London. She observed how people for the most part are disconnected from those they pass by on a day to day basis – the coffee seller, the postman, the *Big Issue* seller outside the tube station, and so on. She was intrigued by Brick Lane, where independent coffee shops and upmarket boutiques rub shoulders with curry houses and flamboyant Bangladeshi market stalls.

Kate wanted to write a piece that somehow highlighted the disparities of a big city. London is constantly evolving, but some of its hurdles remain constant.

THERE IS A man who sleeps in the doorway of the bookshop on Brick Lane. I see him there every evening when I walk home from work, my eyes staring straight ahead, hands ploughed deep into the pockets of my overcoat, with thumping music blaring in my ears. Sometimes he asks for money, his voice thin and frail, but I ignore him and continue to stare ahead. I don't want to miss my train and the station is still a five minute walk away.

I first saw him in the springtime. I had just started working in the area and had yet to get my bearings amidst the labyrinth of graffitied walls and independent coffee shops. The crumbling bricks of yesteryear and gleaming contemporary metal offices vied for space. The smells were all new. Thick, pungent spices and the tang of freshly ground coffee jostled with the stink of rotting litter and cigarettes. Quite a combination.

He was begging for money outside Shoreditch Station. He wore no shoes, just threadbare socks with two filthy, calloused toes sticking out. It was raining and his clothes were sodden, his teeth chattering as he pathetically waved an empty polystyrene cup in the general direction of passers-by. Some people took pity on him and tossed a few coppers his way, but most looked right through him. There are lots of homeless people in London; you can't give money to all of them.

He is an elderly man, thin and malnourished. He has very few teeth, and those he does have are black and rotten. His bright red gums are swollen and inflamed. Probably gingivitis. From beneath a stained khaki beanie, his hair pokes out, shrivelled and coarse like straw. An impressively bushy beard is grey, unkempt, and flecked with spittle and old food particles. His fingers are gnarled and knobbly, fingernails bloody and bitten to the quick. Perhaps he did a lot of manual labour back in the day. Rough palms bear faded scars etched into broken skin. His face is sunken and worn, the flesh tanned to a deep olive from constant exposure to the elements.

The most interesting thing about him is his eyes. They are a startling shade of blue, stormy like the sea and about thirty years younger than the rest of him. They possess a perpetual puppy-like sadness as endearing as it is disconcerting. He wears the same outfit every single day – threadbare brown cords that are stained and ten years out of date, a faded and shapeless check shirt, and a patchy woollen overcoat the colour of swamp-mud. A pungent, musty stench of stale cigarettes, alcohol and piss that you can smell from two meters away clings to him. The stink repels passers-by.

He's not always in the doorway. Sometimes, if I'm out on a lunch break or off to a meeting, I'll see him scrounging through the litter-bins on Shoreditch High Street or gazing up at the street art on Hanbury Street. He mutters to himself in a low, guttural grumble. He walks wearily and with a limp. His left leg appears to be lame. Tourists ignore him. City workers avoid him. They glance at him in disgust if he gets too close, holding their shiny briefcases a little tighter and speeding up their stride. I don't suppose he notices because he doesn't seem all there. He's happy to chat away to himself most of the day.

Once, when I was ordering a round of oozing salt-beef and mustard for the office from Beigel Bake, I saw him in the middle of the street, drunk and ranting at a policeman, with a half-empty bottle of scotch clutched in his left hand. It was a hot summer's day; his face was bright red and dripping with sweat and his top was soaked through at the armpits. He looked quite mad. I exchanged a few half-amused, half-embarrassed glances with the other customers and then lowered my head and pretended not to notice as I marched past, bagels in hand.

He's well known around the area. The café owners often slip him a free latte on cold days. He accepts it with gratitude and nurses it in his crooked hands until the last bit of steam has evaporated. Then he guzzles it down in one.

Tom at the office, a born-and-bred working class boy made good, stops to have a chat with him every so often. Says the old man is one of the old Bow Bell Cockneys, born in Cheapside in the late 1930s just a stone's throw from the church of St. Mary-le-Bow. He's a traditional Cockney, Tom tells me. He says the old man speaks in rhyming slang, and, like half of the East End, claims to be an ex-associate of the Krays. Tom says he's quite switched on, intelligent – when he wants to be. I've seen the old man thumbing through second-hand Dostoyevsky novels on occasion, so I suppose there must be some truth to this. I could never make it past the second chapter of *Crime and Punishment*. Too dense, and too many adjectives for my liking.

Two autumns ago he got into an altercation with another vagrant and spent a week in intensive care. When he came back, his face was a mess. Congealed blood was everywhere, nose broken, eyes swollen and puffy. Half his ear had been bitten off. I felt bad for him, so I gave him a tenner and advised him to spend it wisely. Next time I saw him, he was passed out next to an empty vodka bottle. I shrugged – you can't help some people. Never found out what happened to the other guy, not that I suppose it matters; lots of violence on the streets these days, especially in the East End. Gangs, mostly, but the homeless are a nuisance, too.

It is snowing. Flakes are falling thick and fast, sticking in clumps to my eyelashes and blanketing the discoloured Brick Lane concrete in a film of white. Despite being wrapped in three layers of clothing, I shudder uncontrollably and my hands are stiff with cold. I am walking quicker than usual – the trains don't run for too long in this weather, if at all. I long for the warmth and security of my centrally-heated second floor flat, with an ice-cold Corona waiting to be illuminated when I open the fridge door.

He is in his usual spot, his head resting on the icy pavement, shivering under a thin, woollen blanket. His face is so pale it looks as grey as the ground it is resting on. His eyes have a misty, vacant air that makes him seem as though he is sleeping with his eyes open. On the floor next to his head is a patch of fresh vomit; bright, bilious, and flecked with blood. I hesitate. He really doesn't look well, and I think that perhaps I should phone an ambulance or paramedic. But, I have to get home before the trains stop running. Besides, there are plenty of other people passing by on their way to the station; someone else will call them, I am sure of it.

That was two weeks ago now. I haven't seen him since. No one has. I've asked in all the coffee shops and around the office.

Perhaps he's moved on. Oxford Circus and Angel are quite popular with tramps these days; more suits, more money. Perhaps some Good Samaritan has found him food and shelter; an old folks' home, or maybe the YMCA. Perhaps a long lost relative has tracked him down, cleaned him up and taken him home to live out his last few years in comfort, surrounded by loving cousins, nieces, nephews, grandchildren. Perhaps.

Someone new has taken his place. He's a younger guy with dirty blonde hair and a lopsided grin. Looks like a junkie to me. He asks for money every time I pass, but I ignore him. It's a particularly cold winter and I walk quicker than usual. I have a train to catch.

THAT DAY

JUDITH JOHNSON

ABOUT THE AUTHOR

Judith is a theatre, radio, and TV writer, living in Tower Hamlets. She has been writing short stories for over twenty years. She began writing *That Day* in her creative writing class during a character exercise set in Victoria Park.

When the idea of the child at the centre of Judith's story came to her, it refused to leave. She found it oddly easy to get inside the mind of this character, despite being so much older. It is a sad story, but one that leaves the reader with hope.

I DIN'T HAVE no money that day 'cos my mum din't leave me any by the sink like she would have done normally. I thought she must have forgot, so I had a look in the cupboard to see if there was anything to eat, but there wasn't. There was half a pizza in the fridge, left over from the Saturday, so I ate that.

I thought she was still out, but when I went in the front room, she was lying on the sofa. I started talking to her.

"Alright, Mum," I said. "Where you go last night then? Go to the club again, did you? With the girls? Did you see Aunty Shirl down there? Yeah?"

She din't answer or nothing, but that wasn't anything unusual.

I went out to the Park to see if anyone was around. No one was around by the footy pitches, so I went over by the skate-board ramps. No one round there neither. Too early. So I went and said hello to Bill in the Lodge. He was my mate. But he was too busy; he had to go round in the van picking up the leaves. I said could I come in the van, but he said no, it wasn't allowed. I said it was allowed last week, but he said he wasn't allowed to be on his own with no kids no more. New rules.

I went over to the caff. The Spanish girl was just opening the shutters. They made a real loud sound, hurt my ears.

She said, "Have you had breakfast?"

I lied, din't mention the pizza. I said, "I haven't had nothing to eat since yesterday morning."

She said, "Wait." She went in and got me some bread. It was that brown bread with seeds in it, but she put some peanut butter on it, so it tasted alright.

That caff was better when it did chips and stuff, before they made it all posh. My mum and her mates stopped going there 'cos of that. But the Spanish girl was nice; she was pretty. I was gonna ask for her name the next time I went there, but the next time I went there, I wasn't thinking about her name no more.

I saw Tig by the Lake. My cousin. I ducked quick behind the bushes, but he saw me. Whenever I seen him, my mouth used to go dry and I would feel sick in my stomach. He came over, walking that way he had, like a pimp. "Pimp with a limp," my mum used to say. His skinny white neck had spots all over it, and his eyes had that yellow gunge on 'em, and he had blackheads all over his nose, and his cap still had the price tag on it.

He came over. "Got any fags?" he said.

"Nah," I said.

"Got any food?" he said.

"Nah," I said.

"You better not be lying," he said.

"I'm not," I said. "I swear, Tig."

He went quiet. That was the worse bit, 'cos you could never tell with him. He could switch, just like that. I saw him once, with his dog, his little dog. He was giving it a cuddle like, but his hands were too heavy and the dog come out with a little yelp. Just a little yelp. And Tig picked him up, punched him in the face.

But this time he just walked back a few paces. "See you later, Terminator," he said. Then he limped off.

It started raining then, so I went home.

My mum was still on the sofa.

I went into the kitchen and put the kettle on. I thought, I'll make her a nice cup of tea, she's got hangover. I made the cup of tea, just how she liked it; nice and strong, two sugars. I took it back in the front room with two paracetamols and I said, "Mum, I made you a cuppa." She was lying face down on the sofa, like she does sometimes. Like she did. So I couldn't see the… I couldn't see her stomach. So I still thought she was just asleep.

Her phone went then, in her handbag on the floor. I

stood stock-still and let it ring in case it was the school, 'cos we always ignored the school when they phoned. She din't even stir and I knew something was wrong then, 'cos she always looked at her phone when it rang, case it was some guy. She was always waiting for some guy or other. But this time she din't even move and the ringtone just kept going. Bow Bells it was, like in that nursery rhyme, 'cos we was true Cockneys. Born to the sound of Bow Bells.

When it stopped ringing, it felt like the silence was deafening. My mum was so still, like the Lake in the Park that time it froze over.

I put the cup of tea down on the side table and I tapped her on the shoulder. She din't feel like my mum. She felt like something else, something cold. So I never saw where the knife went in 'cos I din't need to turn her over. I knew.

I went straight round to my Aunty Shirl's. Tig was there, lying on the floor, picking his toenails. I din't want him to know, din't want him to see her like that; I thought he would laugh or something, take the piss. So I asked Aunty Shirl if we could go in the kitchen, but he followed us in there. So when she asked me what was wrong, I din't say nothing. I just asked her if she had any money to buy something for my dinner and she gave me a fiver.

"Ain't your mum got no money left?" she said. "I wouldn't be surprised, she was flashing it around like nobody's business last night."

I bought some chips from the fried chicken shop then I went back to the Park. I thought, "I'll tell Bill," but Bill wasn't in the Lodge; he was still out in the van collecting leaves on his own. So I went back to the caff and I told the Spanish girl. I just said it plain and simple 'cos I couldn't think how else to do it.

"I think my mum's dead," I said. I din't mean to shock her.

She was angry. She thought I'd made it up. "Why you saying horrible things?" she said. She told me to go away.

So I went back home and I sat in the front room, with my mum just lying there, and it sounds stupid but that's when I started talking to her.

I said, "I know people think you been a bad mum to me, but I always loved you. You was full of life. You was funny and we had so many laughs. Like that time we went skate-boarding and you fell on your bum. And dancing to Beyoncé in the kitchen. And not just that, you loved me too. You stroked my head when we watched scary films and I couldn't get to sleep. *Shush,* you said. *Shush now. Everything's gonna be alright.* I know you liked going out, meeting men, having a drink and everything, but you always came home in the end. I always knew you would come home to me in the end."

I know it sounds weird, but I wasn't scared at all. I sat there all night. I got her phone and I went through all the photos, pictures of me and her, right back from when I was little. I talked her through them so she wouldn't forget. I sat on the floor by the sofa and put our favourite DVD on, *Finding Nemo*. I lay down and went to sleep right next to her.

People asked me why I din't call the police, go to a neighbour or something.

Truth is, once we'd settled in for the night, I din't want it to end.

Kelly, the social worker, found me the next morning. She'd been knocking for ages. I ignored her, so she went down the Park to see if anyone had seen me. She knew the Spanish girl from the caff 'cos she'd taken me and my mum there one day and bought us some posh cakes. She came back with the police.

My mum'd bought some man home from the club. Some psycho; she always knew how to pick 'em. They'd had a row. I slept through it all.

I'm living by the seaside now. I got a foster Mum and Dad; they're called Charlotte and Dave – *Chas and Dave*, my mum would've called 'em. My Aunty Shirl said she would take me, but I said no, and Kelly agreed 'cos of Tig being in anger management and all that.

It's nice here. Far from the sound of Bow Bells. I miss her. I miss my mum. But I don't miss nothing else. When I go to bed, I can hear the sea. It makes a noise like, *sshhhh, ssshhh, shush now, shush*. Everything's gonna be alright.

TAKE THE LONG WAY HOME

ANDY MILLWARD

ABOUT THE AUTHOR

Andy is a 50-something freelance management consultant living with his cat in Tiptree, the quiet Essex town famed only for its jam. He is planning a move to France and full-time writing. Divorced and with two children, he comes alive in the pursuit of creativity, including amateur dramatics, social cooking, and a great many twilight hours of writing and honing. Over the years, he has built a portfolio of writing, and he uses his website as a showcase for his many varieties of written work.

Take the Long Way Home was part of a sequence of stories with a twist, in the tradition of Roald Dahl. Andy is drawn to characters that are fumbling with their inner existence, and the main character in this story is a prime example.

IT WAS A clear and decisive moment. I could have taken a direct flight from San Francisco to London, cattle-class, but given my standards in life, I chose not to. I found my mind and body on strike. They resisted in unison, "YOU ARE NOT GOING BACK!"

I can't put my finger on why they disobeyed me. This was an illogical if not downright stupid decision. I could have been home in the UK by lunchtime, alone and snug in my bed. The choice was unequivocal – I was taking the long way home.

Admittedly, thinking of some of my favourite songs helped, starting with the wailing harmonica from a catchy Supertramp tune, followed swiftly by Robert Plant's low moaning tones inviting me to ramble. Rambling was appealing – it would take longer than the time I typically had to spare, to metaphorically journey slowly and find oneself.

It's a cliché from books and movies – a road trip, preferably shared with an oddball companion, finally coming to a realisation about priorities in life and how you're much richer for having taken the journey rather than arriving at the destination.

Well, it's true. I can ask myself why I was in San Francisco and what I was doing travelling back to London, but a more important consideration in any road trip is: What happens next?

I say "road trip," but it doesn't have to be by road; any form of transport can be included. The ultimate destination involves air or sea travel at some point, and the fact I was at an airport predisposed me to at least some initial air travel. But in which direction?

A cough behind me.

There was a further issue to negotiate, since this internal debate occurred while I stood at the airline desk at San Francisco International Airport. Before me sat a girl in a smart, red uniform; fingers poised over a keyboard, ready to action my instructions. Behind me, the queue sounded less happy at my dithering, but somehow, this was an important choice. I knew what I wasn't going to do, I just needed to decide what I *was* going to do.

I drummed my fingers on the desk and smiled with all the "embarrassed Brit" charm I could muster. The girl smiled back politely and cocked her head slightly.

"Er... Can I have a ticket to... to... where would you recommend?"

"Excuse me, sir?"

Her accent told me she was not a West Coast native. Possibly Louisiana?

"Is there anywhere you'd suggest I visit on the way back to England..?"

"I don't know what you're looking for, sir. Maybe you could come back when you've decided..?"

Names popped into my head at random: "Er... Maine? Montana? Montreal? How about Massachusetts? What's in Massachusetts?"

"Well, sir, I can get you on a flight tonight. You'll find guide books in the bookshop. Would that be business class, sir?"

When you are at your least decisive, the dilemmas come thick and fast.

"Actually, forget Massachusetts. I fancy—" I had seen the inviting travel posters, the sorts that hog wall space in every airport on every continent.

If I was slipping off the rails, why not do it in style?

"What's the next flight anywhere in the world you can get me on that doesn't require a visa?"

The girl raised her eyebrows and lowered her gaze to the screen.

"As a British passport holder, I could get you on the flight to... Are you sure you want to do this?"

"Yes. Where is it?"

"Auckland, New Zealand."

"Do it! First class!"

And that was that.

I sat on a plane destined for New Zealand, perversely secure in the knowledge that if the pilot kept flying on and on in roughly the same direction, we'd eventually arrive at the destination I was trying to avoid – London. It's home and it always will be.

For now I can afford to explore the globe at my leisure, my business in San Francisco having been concluded. But, my conscience won't let me forget the inconvenient fact I'm not doing this just because I'm at a loose end, and loaded.

Bet you want to know more about me, don't you? Justin's the name, Justin Smart. It's a smarmy name for which I curse my parents. Quite unlike the man. They say I have a permanent look of half-surprise, but behind the eyes I am a gentle soul. Maybe that's my problem.

Want to know what I am doing in San Francisco?

Well, for want of a better description, I am a courier, the bespoke, be-suited kind who never travels less than business class. I'm a courier who takes personal messages, the kind that can't be transmitted by email or fax. I'm the one they send when it's sufficiently important to deliver a message with gravitas, but where it is not an option for the people behind the communications to deliver it themselves.

Remember Tom Hagen visiting the film producer

in *The Godfather* to make him an offer he couldn't refuse? No, not like that – what my clients do in the comfort of their own corporate glass stumps is up to them. I don't play the grey market. Many do, but I have standards to maintain. I make it a strict condition of business that I am not party to any law-breaking or immorality. In practice, the messages I relay are highly dubious, such that they can cause powerful men to break down and weep like babies. But I remain aloof and independent, as all true professionals should.

Since billion dollar contracts may ride on such messages, naturally I charge a high price for my services. I'm discreet and nobody would dare shoot this messenger – though pride comes before a fall, so I dare not take chances.

There was a time I had flown from London to see a contact I'd met once before. He was wealthy, powerful, and he expected nothing less than the best. Those who failed to meet his exacting standards were airbrushed from his group photos. The meeting had lasted less than five minutes; the message I delivered was contained in one sentence.

He had silently turned to contemplate the San Francisco skyline. I'd had asked if he'd had a reply, but I don't think he'd heard me. Before leaving, I had quietly mentioned that my client would expect a message to confirm his understanding. But, I guessed what might really happen. He would probably wander out on to his penthouse balcony and an hour or so later, his remains would be scraped from the road below by police and ambulance operatives.

I expect this is exactly what my client had hoped for. I imagined he would later search for the news in the *FT* and then smile to himself as he found it.

Nobody would connect this suicide to my client, nor to me, because there was no documentary evidence to link us. The PA would say a suave young British man who left no name or calling card came to visit and was expected, but had left some time before.

Upon my departure, I had heard his request to hold all calls – were they to be his last words? I felt like Edward Fox visiting the OAS top brass in *The Day of the Jackal*.

For this service, I earned £240,000, plus expenses, paid in advance. The expenses were generous, enough to fly me around the world in comfort, the price of silence. My costs appear on the books as "consultancy fees."

The only fly in the ointment is my inevitable and unavoidable return to London.

Meeting the client behind this job is not a problem – if required – although my guess is that he will recommend me quietly in his gentlemen's clubs and then delete my number along with any last traces of remorse. Thankfully, physically deleting me should be strictly off his agenda, although I sometimes worry there may be rogue clients out there. Meeting new clients comes strictly by recommendation, and with careful vetting on both sides.

But I'm procrastinating. If I try and articulate why returning to London is painful, the words, the smooth facade and the years of practice fail me. It would be easy to say, "It's a woman," or, "My mother is dying," or some other platitude, but my relationship with the only place I've ever been able to call home is infinitely complex, not something I can summarise as neatly as the messages I deliver.

It's a dumb line trotted out in a thousand movies, but it's the one lesson I've learned: *everyone has an Achilles heel*. The most successful Teflon-coated people in life can sense weakness and go for the jugular (why is it I always think in clichés?) without fear or hesitation, but they seldom do their own dirty work. I shift in my seat, order a G&T from a chirpy air hostess and for a moment wish I could hire someone else to be in my place. But, I know London is my Achilles heel and only I can do this job.

The fantasy of owning the entire British capital seems rather wonderful. Actually, the specific location of my unassuming two-bed apartment with top notch security and a view of the Thames from a few streets back is the slightly unfashionable end of Docklands, close enough to the action that it's a manageable cab ride to clients in the City. It's probably even within earshot of Bow Bells, if I listen hard enough. The flat is modern and minimal, and resembles a soulless show-home. Mostly I spend my time travelling the world and delivering messages. My wardrobes contain several hand-made suits and shirts for professional purposes. Off-duty, I prefer anonymous chinos and polo shirts that allow me to blend in.

Am I lonely? Well, I do keep to myself, but I also don't mind seeking company, when required. These days, nobody really gets close, not now. When I'm in London, I usually stay around home. When I'm fed up with the sparse décor, I wander outside.

Ask me what I do between client assignments and I will struggle to answer. For some people, life is all about work. When they retire, a yawning gap opens up and they slip into the chasm. You couldn't say that of me. I work whenever the opportunity arises, but it doesn't define me. The difficulty is saying what *does* define me.

Yes, I have my flat, or a pied-à-terre, but I don't have anything to do with my family, don't have a love-life of any description, don't have a motley collection of drinking chums, don't don my Hammers shirt and stand in the crowd on Saturdays bellowing out football songs, don't live the high life, watch theatre, or dine at fine restaurants. In fact, I do nothing conspicuous, but what I do do, I can't honestly tell you. The days slip by all too quietly.

One thing for sure is I live well within my means between jobs. In my line of work, anything obtrusive could get me noticed, and being noticed is not good. The day before my flight to San Francisco, I found myself sitting in Postman's Park, a green corner in the City of London surrounded by tall, evocative buildings, quietly feeding the pigeons.

Not *just* feeding the birds, though. My thoughts wandered to something other than myself. Postman's Park houses the Watts Memorial to "Heroic Self Sacrifice," plaques dedicated to the memory of people who lost their lives saving others. Something about the nobility of such people touches my heart.

I bet that if I lost my life in the line of duty, nobody would raise a plaque. The chances of me rescuing someone from certain death on a railway line or the swirling undercurrents of the Thames are pretty remote, but even if it happened, I would never become a cause célèbre.

Not that I would want to be famous, but some of us are born to occupy the shadows, even in death. If there were an urgent need for me to rescue someone, would I throw myself in the line of fire or simply slink back further into the shadows? There's only one way of knowing, but I'd rather not find out.

If the guy in San Francisco had pulled a gun from his desk and sucked the muzzle like a lollipop, would

I have stopped him? And if so, would it have been out of genuine concern for his welfare and the feelings of his family, or pure self-protection to avoid possible legal ramifications and having to endure police questioning and forensics? No, I do not wish to jeopardise my cover or risk having my passport denied future visas. I would not want blood ruining an expensive suit, and besides, who wants to be confronted with a death you can avoid? Not being a psychopath, it's cleaner and safer for me to slip out the door and leave him to skydive without a parachute by himself.

The business of death doesn't blow my hair back. Creeping home via New Zealand, hopping between a few Pacific Islands, followed by a trip to Tangiers, and then weaving towards Madrid or Venice or Paris or Stockholm, before landing back in London means the dust can settle.

I'm forced to admit there's an element of bullshit to my story. Truth is, I'm also avoiding going home because really I can't stand being alone in London.

Too many bad memories? Not quite. My upbringing was happy enough, dotted around various London boroughs, depending on where Dad could get work. He was a driver; of buses, taxis, limos, lorries, anything – at least until he lost his licence after being caught behind the wheel in an alcoholic haze. Mum worked as a barmaid, the life and soul of the room, but very distant from my life and soul. When Dad went, we drifted apart.

They were salt-of-the-earth, working class people, my past, but not my future. There was me as a barrow boy in my late teens, finding my way in the City, followed by a few office jobs, and then falling into being a messenger. I modelled myself on the types I met in offices and boardrooms. It was a movie that got me started, *The Go-Between*. That was how I saw myself and it was what I became – a middleman for people who needed certain wheels oiling.

All I had to do was copy the behaviour of the top guys, speak their lingo, drop the cheerful cockney banter and talk in a refined, urbane manner that eventually earned their trust.

So that's what I did. I won a reputation for being sound and dependable, got head hunted to do the difficult stuff, and built from there to the point where I was an operator, a freelancer, a metaphorical hired gun, there to communicate things never to be misinterpreted, the kinds of messages that must be relayed with full white-of-eye contact.

My mixers arrive on a small tray along with various accruements. I stare at the oversize ice cubes and tune out the roar of the engines. I'm not all that special, other than I was in the right place at the right time. I made my own luck and did my job well. Clients mentioned me one to another. There was a buzz that

Justin Smart got the right results.

Still, there is London to contend with. Home may be wherever you hang your expensive suits, but so far I've failed to escape London's pervasive emotional tentacles. There is something magnetic dragging me to my roots, much more than familiarity.

If I hate the place so much, why do I continue living there? Most of my clients are international. No reason why I couldn't settle in the States, use a few contacts to pull some jobs. Yes, I know people work all over the world to earn the big bucks, and I could too. Maybe I could earn ten times more, but would it ease my conscience?

It's not as if there is anything I really yearn to spend my money on, nor does it especially motivate me – it's simply an enabler, a baseline. Good suits are merely a uniform, something to wear so the people at the top take me seriously. Hell, I don't even own a car, nor do I take luxury holidays. My work offers all the luxury I could ever wish for.

So what is it about London I despise so vividly, but return to every time like my old man did to firewater? London has not been especially unkind to me. Actually there is much I love about it. Wandering the markets of Camden Lock, Borough, Portobello Road; curry on Brick Lane, discovering musty junk shops and old churches that have remained almost unchanged for centuries. I find solace in ancient graveyards like Bunhill Fields, the last resting place of Jonathan Swift, William Blake, and Richard Cromwell. I like resting on tombstones with a cheese and pickle sandwich and contemplating the world. The more steeped in London's history, the happier I am with myself. When I retire, perhaps I'll become a historian. With London's yesterdays and the city's architecture, I am oddly comfortable. It's the here and now I detest. That, and people.

Yet I feel alive and one with the city's throb when I talk to those hardworking people behind the Indian restaurants and market stalls. But there are some people I loathe – those with facades pretending to be decent while seeming to effortlessly dominate society and business. It's not particular to London, though, is it? You get those sorts everywhere, but it's only this city that gets my goat.

Sometimes, I hate my clients. They're no better than me, but I know better than to bite the hand that feeds me. They love to appear high and mighty, showing off their wealth and routinely dining at stupidly expensive restaurants. I'm not impressed. Some of them are just two steps away from common working class themselves.

And I hate tourists. But then I'm often one myself. Perhaps I'm bitter. Probably a hypocrite, too.

Maybe it's me I can't abide, since I'm pretending to be someone I'm not. I'm not pompous or egotistical, not a political operator, but an actor, sometimes the clown, often the stooge, all froth; straight-talking but without the portfolio.

I should move to the country. Get an old house and do it up, go fishing, become a country squire, find a rosy-cheeked girl to have my babies and only travel to town in the event that clients need me.

But, I know I'd be bored within weeks. Not because I make much use of London's facilities, but because they're there on my doorstep if ever I want them. There's something comforting about knowing I could find an all-night cafe or a dim sum restaurant for those restless nights.

If the city never sleeps, London and I are intertwined. I'm an insomniac before a client engagement and then afterwards I sink into my plush first or business class airplane seat and listen to the throb of the engines. Like now, taking the long way home. When I return to London, my solace will vanish into the traffic fumes and general din.

Truth be told, home usually means watching obscure movies into the early hours and gaming like a teenager instead of sleeping. If I bothered to see a doctor, he or she would probably write a prescription for sleeping pills while showing me the door, but I know it isn't the answer. Meditation, diet, candles, preparing the room for sleep – I've heard it all. It doesn't work and I admit I don't want it to work, either. I fear that when I sleep, the victims of all the messages I've relayed will haunt my dreams. It is daft and irrational for me to fear this, but it has happened, once.

There had been a fat, bearded guy in his early 60s, dressed in a linen suit and a Panama hat. I met him in a cafe in Guatemala City. He was Argentinian and dealt in the import-export trade. My client had been one of his clients, a man with many sidelines, maybe in drugs, arms, money laundering and contraband, but since he had the façade of a legitimate businessman, I knew better than to probe.

The message was coded to thwart my understanding. It's not uncommon for clients to task me with a cryptic message that means nothing out of context – maybe even a quote from the bible or Shakespeare, which cannot be used against me. Most are humdrum but this one was nonsensical. I was told to tell the contact: "Tulip Elephant Bell Comet Orange Violin."

It's not my business to understand messages unless the client wants me to understand and converse with the contact, but this message had bugged me. No matter which way I had turned it, there was no obvious meaning. In vain I had played anagrams with the first letters. It made no sense, and it was clearly not meant to.

And so I had arrived at the cafe by appointment. I identified the contact sitting in the sunshine. I made my introductions and ordered a cappuccino. We had exchanged pleasantries. It was May, which verged on the monsoon season and I had been warned that sudden shelter may be needed.

By the time coffee arrived, the man had become quite jovial and trusting.

Then he had said in good English, "And so to business. I believe you have a message for me?"

I had repeated what I was told, twice in case I made a mistake. I smiled, but his face had frozen. I enquired if he was okay, but his expression had warned me off. Outright fear was etched on his tubby face, branded into his black eyes.

He stood, knocking the table and sending my coffee flying. A nearby waiter had fussed around, but the guy never noticed. His eyes had been fixed on mine as he backed away, and then he turned and run as best his bulk would carry him.

I'm sure he'd made a beeline for the airport and headed straight for Buenos Aires. What had happened next I'll never know, but he visits my dreams – a face that will never leave me.

Afterwards, I'd slept only in snatches for weeks. Then I did something unusual – headed to my local pub and drank gin, neat, all night, until I'd eventually passed out. The following morning I woke in my own bed to a toxic cloud – no idea how I'd got there. I guess I was like a homing pigeon.

A week later, the client took me out for dinner and

had me repeat the story. He laughed out loud – I mean, he *howled* – until I asked what the joke was. Instantly he became serious, shook his head, and put a finger to his lips. He looked at me intently for a moment and whispered, "Stick to the East End, Justin. You're safe there."

Only then did the thunderbolt strike me. The coded message meant something along the lines of, "This man will kill you. Get out!"

Is London a security blanket for me? Being reckless is enticing, but we all have a survival instinct. Like the linen suit, mine requires an exit route in the event of an emergency, but if anyone was going to track me down, London is where they would go looking – and I'm pretty sure I wouldn't run away. They could take me out in broad daylight.

There you go; London is my nemesis, where I will probably meet with fate and never return to tell the tale. It is the city from where I can never truly escape, and for that reason I hate it more than words can say.

But the city is me and I am it. London is where the mask drops. The truth is the one thing I don't want to see or hear.

The truth is this, there is no Justin Smart. He is merely a nametag, a label, a functionary, a toy for clients. At the centre of his existence is a void, and that void is London.

BELLE'S BOWS

MARGARET CROMPTON

ABOUT THE AUTHOR

Although a work of fiction, many elements in this story grew from the author's own experience. Her background is in English literature, social work, and education.

As a young girl, Margaret attended ballet classes and proudly achieved Grade 1 Ballet and Tap. She then moved happily to a retired dancer who didn't bother about examinations, involved everyone in performances and annually took her pupils to Covent Garden. From this teacher, Margaret learnt about kindness, colour and the joy of dancing, however clumsy. Later, she lived and worked in Bethnal Green, near Brick Lane, where she remembers helping some local children put on a song and dance show for the pensioners' club she ran.

Her plays, *The Sellwood Girls* and *When Queen Victoria Came to Tea* (in collaboration with her husband, John), were published in 2015. Other publications include poetry, a children's book, and numerous books, papers and reviews on communicating with children.

This story respects novelist Elizabeth Goudge, who writes with hopefulness and compassion. Margaret feels that she has never danced enough; here, in her first published story (apart from a BBC Radio 4 Morning Story *Gangster's Moll*), she is dancing with words.

MISS ISOBEL BEAUREGARD lived in Cygnet Court, a narrow alley not far from William's Tower, and a little nearer Wren's Cathedral. Her house had once been a grocery store. One great room opened straight from the street, with a tiny kitchen and smaller washroom. Twisty stairs led to her bedroom, shaped like a wedge of cheese, and one other room with a firmly closed door. Beyond the great room was a neat, paved square enclosed by a high wall. Both pavement and wall were almost hidden by tubs, bowls, baskets and pots, all overflowing with colour. There were geraniums and lobelias, daffodils and hyacinths, climbing roses, rosemary, sage and thyme, and an elderly bay tree ever-greening in a corner. In autumn, Virginia creeper glowed scarlet and gold, while in winter, one tall fir stood firm in a scarlet-painted half-barrel.

MISS ISOBEL HAD been christened Bella Bone, but her profession required a more elegant identification.

She had lived nowhere but Cygnet Court and the boundaries of her life were the River Thames, Old Street, Aldersgate, and Brick Lane. Just once, in her long-ago girlhood, had she travelled further.

After her soldier father had been killed in some terrible and far-off war, a kindly grandfather took her to a glittering palace beside an enormous market square that was overflowing with vegetables and fruit. Bella was awed by the plush ruby carpet and crystal chandeliers, as she followed her tall grandfather up a wide staircase to a tiered crescent of seats. As she nervously peered over the shining brass rail, the lights dimmed and she was shocked back into her seat as immense music billowed and bellowed from a deep pit. Then, to her amazement, the crimson wall beyond the pit split in half and disappeared. Ladies in floating white dresses were dancing in the distance.

Bella cried out, "Oh look, Princesses!" but her grandfather whispered, "No, they're swans."

She couldn't at all reconcile this information with the flying birds in her mother's favourite picture, or the long-necked creatures swimming smoothly on the River. Although she couldn't understand them, Bella was entranced by the graceful dancers and enchanted by the glorious music. Perhaps it was inevitable that she should, as she watched Swan Lake at Covent Garden that afternoon, fall in love for the first and last time, and forever. First with ballet, last with the

Prince, and forever with both dance and dancer.

That evening, Bella's mother and the tiny new sister who'd been born while the ballet swans were dying, died too. The kind grandfather moved into Cygnet Court and they did very well together, with the old cat, Jeffery, and new puppy, Cob.

Bella kept the ballet programme in her cardboard box of treasures and looked at the photograph of the Prince every evening before she said her prayers. She longed to be a dancing swan herself and was ready at any time to leap into the lake of death, if she could take that final plunge held tightly in his arms.

When death returned to Cygnet Court, it was the grandfather who died, peacefully together with the very old Jeffery content on his knee. Bella found them both. Once she had grieved and thanked them for their company through her childhood, she entered the next scene of her life.

BELLA LOOKED AS usual at the well-worn ballet programme. She was weary after a long day on her feet serving in the haberdasher's emporium around the corner from Cygnet Court. She was anxious, too. Earlier that day, some customers had been talking; ignoring her while she displayed bolts of fine cloth, matched silks, and lifted down boxes of buttons.

"Such a tragedy!" mourned an over-fed lady. "He fell. Right off the stage. Ruined the scene. Odile was devastated, they say. Her greatest performance destroyed by a clumsy man!"

Her etiolated friend gasped in synthetic sorrow. "And we were to see him tomorrow. I was planning the new turquoise *foulard* with, do you think, the emeralds?"

"Ravishing, my dear, utterly *comme il faut!*"

As Bella looked at the precious photograph, she shivered with worry. Who had fallen? Surely not her Prince! Was he hurt, or safe? How could she find out?

Next morning, Bella called on her friend the tailor, who ate his lunch in the churchyard whenever the weather was clement. Ezra Rosenbaum gathered news from papers discarded by richer readers. There was no doubt. The fallen dancer was her own Prince. He'd twisted his ankle in returning Odile to the stage after a strenuous *pas de deux,* which climaxed with a dramatic lift. His courteous determination to prevent collision with the ballerina had been rewarded with disaster. Turning towards the orchestra pit, he'd slipped too near the edge and plunged, as if into the fatal lake.

Mr. Rosenbaum had heard a rumour that the over-endowed ballerina had carried the persona of the evil enchanter's equally evil daughter into real life. Odile had maliciously pinched the Prince as he pantingly lowered her from the lift, then punished him further with a spiteful elbow to the face as he generously avoided injuring her.

She received sympathy and bouquets. He lay in bed, his leg irremediably damaged, career destroyed.

A week later, Bella asked Mr. Rosenbaum to take a letter to the hospital, where the Prince waited in despair for deliverance. He longed to die, to be released from his evil fate, this death in life. He had no life, no love, no future, no friends, no purpose, no pride. He was nothing, he believed, if his dancing days were done and he could no longer be the Prince. The star whose romantic stage name had been "Alfredo Brunetti" would turn into plain Alfie Brown.

MISS ISOBEL BEAUREGARD'S "House of Dance" skipped with life from the moment the first little girl shyly set a pink-slippered toe to the floor. All day on Saturdays and every weekday from three o'clock until eight, the long room in the old Cygnet Court grocery was transformed into a studio filled with children of all ages and sizes, and both sexes. The only qualification for entry was a desire to dance.

Elsewhere in the city, budding ballerinas pirouetted in high-stepping academies with wall-length mirrors and varnished *barres*, while besotted mothers expended small fortunes in the hope that their tutu-ed offspring *plié-ing* perfectly in all five positions, might one day modestly accept bouquets on some magnificent stage.

In contrast, Miss Beauregard's fees were minimal and not always paid, but no child was ever turned away and payment always came in some form, perhaps fruit or flowers, a knitted scarf or a crisply crusted pie. The most precious rewards were the delight of the dancers and their parents' gratitude. Isobel's continued service in the haberdashery emporium maintained the household.

Lessons lasted for forty minutes, plus ten for arriving and changing into ballet shoes. Afterwards, there was always a refreshing drink and a moment to stroke the cats, Florizel and Aurora. Return to the everyday world began a long week before the next hour of magic.

The teacher was a tall, handsome man with a limp. He was patient and gentle with everyone, however plodding and clumsy. He taught that spontaneous grace is achieved only through careful discipline and he was brisk with children who were lazy or deliberately impeded others.

The teacher was always addressed as "Mr. Prince", but his elegantly foreign accent hinted at an origin far to the east of Cygnet Court. He had once been famously known by a more intriguing name, but he never referred to those days. He had no need. Every inch of wall in the narrow corridor at the old grocery, now known as "The Swan's Nest", was covered with photographs and old programmes, a panoramic biography of the dancer known as "Alfredo Brunetti", whose flamboyant career had been precipitously curtailed. Alfredo, who had captured young Bella's heart as the Prince, now lived in Cygnet Court under a different, plainer name. At night he slept on a canvas camp bed in the studio.

Ezra Rosenbaum played the music to accompany the young dancers on an elderly, upright piano with faded violet silk behind its fretwork and with tarnished, brass candleholder at either side of the music-stand. After each class, Isobel, Ezra, and Alfie shared supper, and talked about the many engrossing matters concerning ballet.

One evening, Alfie said, "They call you Miss Bow. Do you mind?"

Isobel looked pleased. "Some of the children have been asking me to put on a show for their parents."

Ezra clapped his hands. "They said to me, could they dance for the old people at the church club—"

"—In the parish hall, where there's a little stage and a piano and plenty of chairs," Isobel interrupted.

"And they asked if they could be a real company and have a stage name, and I said I'd have to ask you both, but I thought—" Isobel and Ezra stopped in mid-flight and turned to the silent teacher.

He smiled slowly. "Yes, why not? It is time."

"And the stage name?" Ezra and Isobel spoke together and laughed.

Some nearby church bells rang for the hour.

"Of course," said Alfie, "how about, Miss Bow's Bells?"

Isobel looked doubtful while Ezra scratched his eyebrows. "Miss Belle's Bows? No, Belle's Bows!" he said.

Alfie applauded: "Not just a show. Isobel, Ezra – we'll make a new ballet."

Ezra waved in excitement. "I will arrange the music."

Isobel blushed with delight. "We'll need costumes and props."

Alfie said quietly, "We can use my old costumes. It's foolish to waste a whole room as a wardrobe, after all. And I was wondering Isobel, now I can walk so much better, might I move my bed into that room? I'm sure I could climb the stairs."

Isobel smiled, "Of course, my dear. The room is yours. I'll buy you a proper bed. We can store costumes in boxes along the walls in here, and use the tops as seats. And I'll ask Mr. Furbelow for offcuts of fabric, ends of rolls, damaged lace and snippets of trimmings."

Ezra stood to announce, "My sister Naomi is a fine needlewoman. You may be sure she would love to make beautiful, bright clothes for our dancers, to be part of the show. She used to dance. And sing. But when her heart was broken, she could not find her life anymore. She has not sung for many years."

WHEN ALFIE AND Isobel had been born, Bow Bells could be heard far over the roofs of London, to the north and east. They proudly realised that they were both fully qualified Cockneys. The foreign accent Alfie had acquired during his glittering dancing days all but disappeared and returned to the natural tones of his native neighbourhood. Although Ezra had been born in a distant country, he no longer thought of London only as a refuge. He was home.

London Bells celebrated the few square miles of the East End surrounding Cygnet Court. The new ballet was, Alfie said, his greatest success; greater than any performance on the famous stages of the world where, in a different life, he had partnered superlative prima ballerinas.

Ezra's sister taught the children to sing with confidence and joy. She recovered her voice and her delight in life as she created a miracle of colour and design from the overflowing boxes of princely costumes and haberdashery morsels. Mothers, grandmothers, aunts and neighbours cut, fitted, embroidered and stitched – thrilled to be part of this wonderful adventure.

Every dancer had a part that was perfectly crafted to suit their individual ability. Even stolid, silly Lulu shone as the Great Bell of Bow, flat feet firmly grounded as she swayed plump arms almost in time to the resounding piano chords. Three-year-olds in bright overalls tinkled tiny rattle-bells as they skipped in a circle, and all fell down together in a cheerful round of *Ring-a-Roses,* with its alleged homage to the Plague. Lithe, quick, black-skinned Lucetta chased them off the stage, flickering, leaping, blazing, with her enveloping scarlet draperies flying. As the Great Fire of London, she destroyed everything within reach, including the Plague itself, then sank to the floor and was blown as embers into the wings. Elegant twins, Abdul and Habiba, mimed Dick Whittington being encouraged by his velvet-suited cat, while sweet-voiced Bows entreated him to "turn again!"

For the finale, boy Bows robustly pulled down apples from the tree on Saint Paul's steeple and then ran from hedge to hedge until they came to London Bridge. Girls posed as tree, steeple, hedge and bridge, and chanted the rhyme. Once London Bridge had been reached, all the children joined in a joyous country dance, *Gathering Peascods*, to remind themselves and their parents that London was a series of villages, never far from its rural roots. The old people in the audience needed no such reminder.

THE BOMB HIT when Alfie and Isobel were asleep, safe in their nightly dreams of dancing. Alfie revelled in memories of his life as the Prince, lifting an exquisite ballerina in the form of Isobel, who lay peacefully in the next room. Isobel's sleep was happy, too, as she again became young Bella, supported in a perfectly balanced *arabesque* by her loving Prince. Aurora and Florizel purred, one on each bed.

WHAT WAS LEFT of Cygnet Court became a place of beauty. Plants flourished in ruined walls and pavements. A pool formed in a small crater. In a sheltered corner, Ezra and Naomi placed old chairs that had been rescued from other lost homes. Former dancers, some in the armed services, others bravely maintaining everyday life in the broken streets, came to the peaceful garden and remembered their youth, and hoped.

When it was rebuilt, the garden with its little pond was included in the design. There would be no more odd-shaped dwellings or twining lanes, but office blocks allowed access to a courtyard, where workers brought lunchtime picnics, enjoying inspiration for new projects, and relief from their anxieties.

In a new century, these blocks were despised as too small and old-fashioned. Great glass towers now reflected sun, sky and clouds dancing across vast, vertical, mirroring lakes. Despite the demand for workspace, the fashionable architect incorporated a curving green space in the centre of the complex.

No bombs dropped, but the agonies of mental torture within the glass shells echoed the physical pains of ancient prisoners in the nearby Norman Tower. Yet the peace of that garden was never disturbed. Everyone who sat by the elegant fountain in its white-stone-surrounded lily pond experienced unexpected delight, and an inexplicable impulse to dance.

THE FIRST CYGNET Court Festival was created by redundant IT specialist, Izzy.

The anonymous managerial email snapped: "Yr contract ends F'day. Sorry." Izzy cleared her locker of the few possessions permitted: mug, umbrella, cosmetics and washing kit. She then subsided onto the low wall beside the courtyard pool. Hardly able to see through a film of tears, her attention was deflected from misery by the shimmering fountain. A glint of hope plumed into a torrent of excitement. She had an idea. Instead of wasting energy on fruitlessly seeking further employment in the cloud of bits, bytes and screens, she recklessly spent her redundancy money on rent and food, and set out on a new adventure. Izzy gathered a flock of friends who had, like her, abruptly acquired too much free time.

"We must dance!" she commanded. "We can help everyone to dance."

She chose the anniversary of the first "Belle's Bows" concert. Her great-grandmother, the former Great Fire of London, had told Izzy the story. Lucetta had given the little girl the fragile scarlet scarf she'd worn on that magical day. Lucetta had continued to dance until, attaining a century, she had blazed out of her body while enthusiastically teaching Zumba.

On that Festival Day, the usual tranquility of Cygnet Court was replaced by excitement, sound and movement. Yet, it remained a place of peace. From dawn until midnight, the pavement became a dance-floor. Musicians competed to provide lively or languorous rhythms and melodies. Highly-trained groups performed programmes from many traditions. Individuals played pipes, fiddles and the rickety pianos which had been wheeled into corners and archways. Everyone danced, celebrating life and hope.

Dancing overflowed onto surrounding streets and drew passers-by, who forgot where they had been passing to, or why. Patrolling police and hoody-hidden drug-users danced with bag-laden shoppers and service-bound clerics. Twirling children skipped and leaped, while swaying elders zoomed their Zimmer frames. Four dancers were present, as always, but never seen. No longer restrained by age or injury, physical infirmity or lost confidence, Alfie and Bella, Ezra and Naomi, lived as they had always loved, in the pure spirit of dance.

THE SQUARE

CLARE HURST

ABOUT THE AUTHOR

Clare grew up in Cambridgeshire, and now lives in East London. One of her favourite pastimes is discovering odd pockets of London.

The idea for this story was formulated during her early morning walks to the tube. Against the backdrop of seemingly endless bad news in the media and new housing developments popping up everywhere in London, she wondered what the houses made of it all.

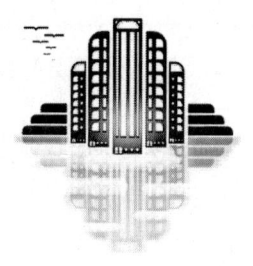

THE HOUSES ON the Square know long before the humans do. Number 23 sets off the alarm. The solitary boy who had taken her attic studio a few months ago has begun to collect things.

Number 23 knows something is up, but isn't sure exactly what. She nudges her neighbour, sending creaks and whisperings down the west side of the Square. Time and traffic fumes have turned the once-sandy brickwork in this corner of East London to burnt toffee. Despite the peeling paintwork and bags of uncollected rubbish on doorsteps, the row of terraced townhouses retain a certain solemn elegance.

At the nudge of Number 23, mice scamper between ancient walls and balls of dust drift out of long-forgotten corners. In the kitchen of Number 25 a precariously balanced wine glass slips and shatters. Shadowy brickwork arches over dark and impassive windows outside, imperceptible to human eyes.

"What's he up to?" reverberates along the row.

On reaching the corner, the question bounces off some overhanging trees nearby and then echoes back and forth between the eastern and western terraces in the Square. Finally, the new-builds on the northern edge pick up the question, and nervously flip it between each other.

Almost as an afterthought, the question is flung to the low-rise blocks and garages on the southern perimeter. There are no mock period features or elegant wrought-iron balconies there. A different kind of aspiration is reflected in those north-facing beacons of a now-lapsed modernity. It's all about clean lines and functionality. Dreams of a better world waver hopefully above obvious signs of petty vandalism and disrepair in this network of open walkways and homely front doors.

Unobserved by the Square's human inhabitants, the boy quietly comes and goes. Sometimes, he leaves the house at dawn for twenty minutes and then returns, shaking. On other occasions, he disappears for several days like a wayward cat, slinking back late at night with fresh prey – heavy loads of books or odd little packets and tubes bundled up in plastic bags.

A call to arms is issued from Flat 8b, Futura House, the largest of the council blocks. She is a constant battleground between landlord and tenants, and she will not sit back apathetically in the face of such outrage; especially not Flat 8b. Her tenants are slightly unusual, having chosen their dwelling for reasons of principle rather than economy. Several nights a week the rooms are filled with similarly principled friends, where ideological arguments and equally ideological cooking smells seep into the walls and under the front door. The elderly Pakistani couple next door retaliate by slow-cooking the spiciest Karahi recipes they know of early on Saturday mornings. Other neighbours and their dogs are more vocal in their disapprobation.

"We must act," announces Flat 8b.

"We've endured two world wars, floods, earthquakes, and the great storm of '87. Our code is dignity and silence. That's the way of this Square," Number 25 replies. He is one of the oldest and most respected houses. His foundations are said to overlie a much older dwelling. Ancient timbers marked with curious etchings and the nibblings of long-dead woodworms are grafted into his structure. His rather smart new owners (doctor, lawyer, and baby) have aptly repainted his outer woodwork a glossy statesman-esque grey.

"He's building a bomb," says Number 23.

A moment of silence follows.

"I don't know why no one is saying it out loud. It's perfectly clear. Look at what he brings back in his rucksack each day: chemicals, powders, batteries. Not your average student shopping list," says Number 23.

Number 11 unsettles the other buildings with his dirty, peeling and boarded-up exterior. Inside, he is overrun with spiders and a strange, changing community of pale, unhealthy-looking humans. Usually, he maintains a slightly glazed and unnerving silence, which he now supplies.

"He spends hours on his computer," Number 23 says, ignoring Number 11's stare. "I know the words he writes: nitroglycerin and triacetone triperoxide. Take my word for it, I've heard of some chemicals in my time and those aren't the types you want in your rafters."

"But why would anyone want to destroy us?" The south-facing new-builds are incredulous.

Mutterings come from other corners of the Square: "Typical, ignorant newcomers; haven't they ever seen the news?"

"Who cares," grumble the garages. "We're being knocked down and turned into a seven-story block of flats next year. We're doomed anyway."

An awkward orangey-brown flush creeps over the new builds.

A glare from Number 25 silences everyone. "We must stand together," he says. "Unified. Some of you are too young to remember, but once Winston Churchill visited this Square. Just like now, when destruction was in the air; people were firing guns, the place was swarming with police and panic was everywhere. Mr. Churchill stood just over there in a top hat and fur overcoat. He told everyone to stay calm, to hold on, and that he would bring the perpetrators to justice."

There are shufflings of assent. Number 32 above the newsagents is not really part of the Square, but she pokes her nose in whenever anything interesting is afoot. "Too right. I remember it, bullets flying up the street. Dangerous criminals on the loose. The humans even called it a siege. But did we panic and break our code? No, we stood our ground, like we must today." Having said her piece, she settles back into place. Glimpses of bright furniture and flowered curtains flutter through her open windows.

Since they spruced her up and divided her into flats, that Number 32 has become unbearably smug, reflects Number 9. Perched on the southeast corner, he is still owned and inhabited by a proper East Ender. Born and bred, a true-blue Bow Bells baby – if such a thing still matters to anyone these days. Number 9 is proud of his pedigree, of the authenticity of the faded wallpaper and memories that lurk behind his fly-spotted net curtains. "I'm with you on this one, Guvnor," he says with a gruff nod. He retreats to his comforting smoky smells and racing on telly in the front room.

At that moment, the boy slopes into the Square on

his bike. He's young, tentative and unassuming. The buildings square up to him, a David and Goliath tableau that goes almost unnoticed. Bending down to lock his bike onto the railing outside Number 23, the lad suddenly senses he's being watched. He looks up. No one is there of course, only the usual sights and sounds of the Square. An ambulance siren wails somewhere on Whitechapel Road, a television is on full volume in the ground-floor flat, and building work carries on down the road where another new development is being drilled and cranked into existence.

Number 23 had felt maternal towards the boy when he'd first moved into her cramped, top-floor quarters. Once upon a time, the building had been overflowing with tenants and their families. It wasn't right having so many people crammed into her rooms, she'd though. Fortunately, that hadn't been the case since. Nowadays, a Bangladeshi family resides on her first floor, with another family on the second. She quite likes their strict and tidy ways. The same can't be said for her other inhabitants – a middle-aged man in a wheelchair with his live-in carer on the ground floor, and an overweight and rather morose lady in the basement. Neither receive many guests and the latter positively discourages them, spending most of her days dragging a wheelie-suitcase around Watney Market, where she mutters racist comments at the stall-holders and occasionally buys a cauliflower or cabbage ("proper English vegetables, thank you very much"), before meandering back to her basement. An unusual, if not slightly dysfunctional bunch; far removed from how things were when all of her floors were united.

The waif-like lad somehow managed to tug at Number 23's crossbeams. At the time he had moved in, she had been in the habit of eavesdropping on the Bangladeshi father, who reads stories to his sons each evening. Then, he had been terribly keen on an antiquated notion of the British education system. His preference had been for books involving boarding school hijinks, which his well-behaved sons considered baffling and dull, and they had suffered silently through their father's nightly readings. More recently, and to the boys profound relief, their father discovers Harry Potter and the nightly readings now gain a warmer reception, despite everyone's privately held reservations as to whether the books actually provide any useful clues for acquiring the swaggering old Etonian confidence of politicians, as seen on television.

The boy in the attic actually reminds Number 23 of Harry Potter – alone, pale, and set apart from others. Perhaps she has turned a blind eye for too long. Though bound by an unwritten code of non-interference, buildings occasionally permit themselves the tiniest of infringements; a sleepless night of creakings and murmurings for an errant husband, or a suddenly fused light bulb in the midst of a family row.

Number 23 sets about observing the boy's comings and goings more carefully. She is waiting for the ideal moment to make a small interference to divert him from the path of annihilation he seems bent on.

She watches the boy pore over maps and diagrams late at night. She describes the strange geometric designs to Number 25, who gravely deems them "maps of the city's underground system."

"The veins and arteries of the city," he opines with a creaking growl that wakens the lawyer-doctor-baby family.

Number 23 watches as the boy's eyes are glued to his computer screen for hours on end. The lad makes notes, and occasionally he takes items from a hoard hidden under a floorboard. Small, chemical concoctions are mixed, making tiny sparks that fly up to her rafters.

She watches the boy take out photographs of a man and a woman. She watches him sob silently without releasing a single tear. And then she watches him cut the photos up and burn their fragments slowly, one by one.

The skittish new-builds do their best to pretend

nothing is wrong. Their clean window panes sparkle in the sunshine as they compare notes on their new owners and boast about their deluxe new kitchens.

But the others grow serious. The ground floor of Futura House and a neighbouring block band together in military-style units. 8b becomes an authority on foundations and structure, and the impact of explosions on particular types of postwar concrete and design. The older houses creak and groan uneasily.

I must do something, thinks Number 23. Somehow that moment never comes. For a whole week, she eyes a heavy glass jar perched precariously on a shelf above the boy's bed, wondering whether she could tilt it just enough to dislodge it. She imagines the jar crashing on the boy's forehead as he sleeps.

"Probably a storm in a teacup," whispers Number 28. "Why would he bother blowing up our little Square? Terrorists go for targets. Big buildings, underground stations, landmarks. We've got the Tower of London on our doorsteps for goodness sake – why would he bother with us?"

"That's not the point! What about those buildings?" argues Number 27.

"What if he has an accident? Mixes them powders wrong one night, then *boom*. End of us there and then." Number 23 has seen too much.

The boy looks paler than before. He spends even

longer holed up with his collection of chemicals. The small explosions are getting bigger. Sparks and detritus are contained in a cast iron safe he has somehow managed to lug inside under the cover of pre-dawn darkness, from a skip.

He seems close to executing his plan. But what is the plan? Number 25 observes the lawyer-doctor's evening newspaper with its depressing reports of high school massacres, marathon bombings, and someone stabbed in broad daylight, just down the road.

"Death and destruction – humanity's response to the absurdity of temporary existence," Number 25 mutters knowingly to himself.

The seasons turn to autumn and a heightened silence reigns in the Square. The boy is ready. Or rather, *it* is ready.

One day, he packs up his alchemist's hoard. Puts it all neatly away in the safe. Everything else, not that there is much more, goes into one small suitcase. He places the safe under the floorboards and leaves the house with the suitcase.

"He's gone?" the house whispers.

"He's gone," they sigh with relief.

"But what about…?" Number 32 starts to say.

"Best not think of it anymore, all that stuff hidden away. We'll be safe now. Safe as houses," replies Number 25.

Someone new is moving in.

A girl brings rack upon rack of clothes, books and pictures. She has friends dropping in all hours of the day and night. The tiny studio room is crammed. People chatter on the phone inside and outside. They laugh and play music. There is no dark anguish swirling in this one's skull. The loose floorboard languishes untouched under mountains of clothes and magazines.

Then she's gone, and another human moves in, and so on, until the lonely boy and his nocturnal tinkerings are a thing of the past. Number 23 particularly likes the Swedish musician, who plays the guitar and seduces girls with offers of Swedish massages and his specialty dish, a one-pot stew cooked on the tiny hob. The massages never quite materialise once the girl has shed her top. In the mornings, he sits alone and naked on the floor, happily finishing the cold stew straight from the pot with last night's dirty cutlery, absent-mindedly wiggling the loose floorboard with his toe.

Number 23 is calm these days. When the news arrives that her inhabitants are to be evicted and that she will be renovated from top to toe, she remains unflappable. In fact, she is secretly pleased. She imagines her shiny new self, superior to the no-longer-so-pristine new-builds. But she cannot envisage the machinery, the tearing and the drilling it will take. She cannot foresee that the owner's interior designer will notice the large, disused space beneath the attic floor. He will want to create an atrium for relaxation, achieved by knocking through the second floor ceiling. She happily imagines the estate agent's patter, "A charming Georgian townhouse sympathetically restored with contemporary finishes. Excellent transport links. Would suit a professional family."

It's an autumn afternoon like many others before, and the Square is quiet. Suddenly a woman and two small children burst into view. The children run ahead, kicking leaves and shrieking merrily. The woman runs after them, also laughing. It seems the Square is not their destination. She stops, consults a map and turns back.

"We're lost!" she shouts.

Around the corner emerges a slight, handsome man, brushing dark hair from his eyes. The four figures have the chocolate-box glow of a happy family.

"Let me have a look – what's the name of this Square? I used to live in this part of town, ought to be able to find my way," the man says. He peers over the woman's shoulder at the map.

"Wait, this must be... this must be the Square I lived in, just after I first moved to London. Just after my parents…"

She is squeezing his hand. "You poor thing," she says. "How tough to be alone in London for the first time. Still, what a beautiful place to live, so smart! Which building did you live in – one of these lovely old townhouses? In some charming little garret up the top? Surely not one of these swanky concrete and glass penthouses?"

The man's eyes have clouded. "Right first guess."

"How fun, which number?"

A pause. "Number 23."

"Come on, kids, race you to Number 23 – where Dad used to live!"

She hands him the map and then three figures run across the Square, coats flapping, leaves scattering.

Dad hangs back, taking in the scene; new houses boasting shiny sheets of glass and concrete to replace the grimy old council blocks. A trendy deli is situated on the corner where the shabby old newsagent once stood. Neat flowerbeds are in the main Square, and, directly opposite, a row of beautifully restored dark-brick townhouses resemble a row of teeth. A polished, modern building stands out, like an incongruous gold filling.

"But that's strange…" He consults the map again, just to be sure. "Number 23 is brand new."